The Half-Pipe Kidd

The Half-Pipe Kidd

Alison Acheson

COTEAU BOOKS

This novel is a work of fiction. Names, characters, places, and incidents either are the product of the author's imagination or are used fictitiously. Any resemblance to actual persons, living or dead, is coincidental.

Edited by Barbara Sapergia.

Cover painting by Ward Schell.
Cover design by Ed Pas.
Typeset by Karen Thomas.
Printed and bound in Canada.

The publisher gratefully acknowledges the financial assistance of the Saskatchewan Arts Board, the Canada Council for the Arts, the Department of Canadian Heritage, and the City of Regina Arts Commission, for its publishing program.

Canadian Cataloguing in Publication Data

Acheson, Alison, 1964-
    The Half-Pipe Kidd
    ISBN 1-55050-120-8

I. Title.

PS8551.C32H34 1997   jC813'.54   C97-920091-1
PZ7.A33Ha 1997

COTEAU BOOKS
401-2206 Dewdney Avenue
Regina, Saskatchewan
S4R 1H3

Available in the United States, from:
General Distribution Services Inc.
85 River Rock Drive, Ste 202
Buffalo, NY 14207

this time for Ole, too

table of contents

dare

I ENTER THE CONTEST ON A DARE. Roland makes me do it.

"Hey, this is a good poem, Og!" He reads the words aloud but doesn't get past the third line, and I grab it out of his spiney fingers and throw it back in the pile of math papers on top of my desk.

"But it's good!" he insists. "When you have a talent like that, you've got to do something about it."

"It's not a talent."

"But it is. Just like your freestyle riding is a talent, and my...." He waves his hands in the air. "My...." He shrugs.

"Your straight A's," I say.

He grimaces and strokes the navy tie around his neck.

"My ability to tie a necktie." He picks up the poem again, reads it once more. "Really, Kidd, you've got to do something with this. You can't let it rot away." His voice has an intensity I haven't heard before.

"Whatever." I take the paper from him again and this time push it into a drawer and slam it shut. "It's not important."

"But it is." Now he's pulling on his necktie.

"It's nothing to be so excited about, Roland. Forget it!"

Finally he's quiet. But he doesn't forget it. He remembers it the day Ms. Potter makes me read in English class, and that's the same day she announces that the local rag—as Mum calls it—is sponsoring a poetry contest for students.

He passes a note to me in class, something he hardly ever does. *Go for it, Kidd!* And when I shake my head, he actually says aloud: "I dare you."

I shake my head again and whisper, "No."

Then he says the magic words.

"You do, and I'll buy you a piece of plywood for the half-pipe. You win and I'll buy you two!"

Okay. Even one piece of plywood will help. "You're on!" There's nothing to lose. I can't possibly win, and no one will ever know I've written that stupid poem—except for Roland, of course, and he'll be busy down at the lumberyard picking up a sheet of plywood!

Ms. Potter is clearing her throat. "Are you both through? School will soon be over and you can be off on your bikes then. Really, Roland. I don't expect this of *you*." But she gives me a look. I guess I don't surprise her at all.

I look at Roland and he's got his private-school-flush happening; at least, that's what Couch and I call it. Roland hates being reprimanded in class. He tries to be cool about it, but his face turns kind of red. I try not to hassle him about it now, but Couch still does.

Ms. Potter turns her back to us, goes on about the contest, and writes the address on the board.

Roland gives me a quick look and his eyes are strange—kinda rolling and wild, as if he's an animal caught. Then he turns quickly away and copies down the address from the board, which he doesn't have to do, because the clunky old mailbox of *The Optimist* is right around the corner from where I live. I watch him, his back hunched, his hand tight to the paper as he writes. I have a sudden urge to pat his shoulder, tell him it'll be all right.

MS. POTTER STOPS BY AND TAPS MY DESK with the piece of chalk she always has in her hand. "Where is Chester today?"

"Couch?"

"Chester. Where is he?"

"He's not here."

She bends down, pretends to wipe dust off his seat. Then she gives me The Look. She thinks I do know where Couch is; I'm just not saying.

I look right back at her. You can't expect a teacher to understand that some people just aren't excited about school.

Ms. Potter stares right back at me. "You let Chester know that I'll be sending him to visit Mr. Trevitt...."

At this moment, Mr. Trevitt's voice comes over the P.A. "Hello?" he always begins, as if we're going to answer him. Somebody usually does shout "hello" back.

"Hello?" he says again. "I'm pleased to announce the winners of the poetry contest sponsored by *The Optimist* newspaper...."

I begin to dig through my knapsack for that novel we were supposed to read. Mr. Trevitt goes on and on. I think he'd rather be a radio announcer than a principal.

"The winning poems will be published in tomorrow's edition and posted on the office door...."

Then I hear my name.

"Second prize goes to our own Ogilvie Kidd!"

No!

Ms. Potter drops her chalk. She doesn't look at me until after she's picked up the four pieces, even the little chip under Mallory Nightingale's desk.

"Well. Ogilvie," she says. "I didn't know you're a poet. Congratulations." She holds out her hand.

I shake it. I've never had a teacher congratulate me before. I'm glad Couch is missing another English class.

"You must bring it in and read it for us." Ms. Potter moves, and I see Mallory, two seats ahead, staring at me.

She probably entered the contest; it's the sort of thing she'd do. Then she smiles at me.

I turn away and there's Roland, with a grin like a half-moon. "I knew it! I owe you two pieces of plywood!" he says aloud.

Yeah—plywood. The silver lining in this cloud.

The cloud: Mum and her not-so-secret desire to have an artist-child.

For a moment I wish with every cell of my body that my poem won't be published.

Maybe I can hide the paper.

No chance. It's spring, and every weekend it's Garage Sales—I always think of it as Mum's Garage-Sailing. She circles every ad in the classifieds, then off she goes on her bike. Sometimes she has to call for a cab to fetch the stuff. That's when it gets pretty bad around the house: garage full of furniture pieces, the smell of dissolving varnish and musty chesterfield stuffing, and in the kitchen, the sound of the sewing machine screaming around piping-edged corners of upholstery fabric.

Back to the poem.

Now it's going to start again. Mum peering over my shoulder every time I pick up something to read. Even if it's just the *TV Guide*. Especially if it's just the *TV Guide*.

My grandpa was a poet, so Mum's always had this funny thing about me. Even the fact I'm left-handed makes her all excited, as if because of *that* I must have some incredible artistic streak or something.

I have a picture of me when I was three months old, and there she is, sticking a book in front of my face, waving at the camera. Okay, so maybe I was looking at the book. Does that make me a genius? I probably liked the pictures. I *still* like the pictures, except now I'm fifteen and in my last year of junior high.

I look up and Mallory Nightingale's still looking at me. It's not a bad look. She turns away, and I can see the back of her head, her light brown hair, so fine I can see her scalp. It has a bit of a curl—a flip here and there really, not curl—and it reminds me of the bird's nest I found last spring near the Fraser River. Soft, sweet-smelling cottonwood down, woven into a cup of twigs and straw. It tickled my nose when I held it to have a closer look at the speckled egg chip left behind.

5

Some of the guys, Couch for one, tease Mallory about her hair, but I don't. Not because I'm a nice guy, but because I kind of like it. Her head is small and round, without any of the lumps I feel on my own head when I'm shampooing. At least, I don't think so. Her head doesn't look lumpy. I can imagine what the feathery strands feel like, but I'd like to touch her hair just once and really know.

Whew! I shake my head.

Man, I'm glad Couch is missing English today.

A HALF-PIPE IS A WOODEN PLATFORM constructed with plywood and two-by-fours. There are quarter-turn ramps at either end, and these ramps rise into the air about three meters, and at the top of each there's a narrow platform with a railing. The idea is to ride from one end to the other—building speed— and get some air under you off the top. I can go up each ramp and do 180 degree turns and tailwhips...almost. The platform at the top is kind of like a breathing space. You fly up there and stop, watch the other guys, or think about your next trick.

When I started, what I was most afraid of was coming off the top. It was okay to ride and fly, ride and fly, twisting at each end, but when it came to stopping up there and then starting again, throwing myself and the bike into the ramp and trying to stay in control so I'd land properly and not lose the bike, that was scary. Sometimes I felt like the bike was going to drop out from under me. And there was the time I landed...kind of funny, if you know what I mean. Mum made me go to the doctor because I made the mistake of telling her about it.

But I got used to the dropping-in thing, and now I can't believe it ever bothered me.

I guess you can get used to anything if you do it often enough. Which is why I'll never get used to this prize-winning stuff. That poem happened when I was supposed to be doing my homework, one day in February when there was about forty centimeters of snow out on the half-pipe, and the yard outside my window was quiet for a change. Usually it's a constant hum of wheels and the sound of drop-thud, drop-thud, and I guess I was thinking about that—thinking how to describe it—and there was my notebook—my math notebook—and there was already a pen in my hand.

Maybe Roland can think of some way of hiding it from Mum.

"I've got to hide it," I tell him. "Any bright ideas?"

"Your mum will be cool about it," he says.

"I know," I say. "She'll be *too* cool. It's what she's always wanted."

"But you are going to surprise her, and she *is* going to be cool," he says, as if that's all that matters.

"What would happen if you surprised your mum?" I ask.

Roland doesn't pause with his answer. "Oh, she'd have a conniption. That's what she always says—a conniption." He laughs, one big HA! But I don't think I'm supposed to laugh with him. Then he's serious and thinks for a minute—a long minute, while Mr. Allman explains something about the Crow's Nest Pass railway agreement—and all he can come up with is, "Pretend you didn't write it."

Can you believe it? Pretend I didn't write it? Who else would write a poem about freestyling?

But I begin to think about Roland's idea on the way home, pushing Mum's ten-speed, or Tin-Speed as I call it, that once again has fallen apart. This time it's the chain. I'll need a chain breaker to fix it when I get home. (Mum abandoned this thing when she bought an enormous three-wheeler with a basket on the back—her tricycle.)

The more I think about Roland's idea, the more sense it makes. After all, if *I'd* written a poem about freestyling, why couldn't someone else? I'm not the only half-pipe freak around. It could've been anyone.

I imagine Mum as I think this: she'd have *The Optimist* in one hand and her sewing scissors in the other, and she would jab at the paper with the scissors. "Look! Your name—right here. Ogilvie Kidd. That's you, isn't it?"

"That's my name," I'd say, but this big question mark would float around our kitchen.

Mum might peer at the paper. "That is your name." But the question mark would settle nicely around her shoulders and she just might sound a bit doubtful. And begin to look slightly horrified.

She'd whisper. "There isn't another Ogilvie Kidd around, is there?"

"No, Mum." And I couldn't help it—I'd laugh, because I've heard over and over how she didn't name me for weeks, not until she found a name that she thought no one else would have.

"It is a good name, isn't it?" I would ask her.

"It is. It took me fourteen and a half weeks...."

Every time I hear the story, it takes longer and longer to name me.

"In fact, it's such a great name that someone decided to borrow it, Mum." That's what I could say.

There'd be a minute of silence, and in that time I'd hope—in vain—that she'd not ask anymore questions.

"*Borrow* it!"

No, this wouldn't work at all; who'd borrow a name like Ogilvie Kidd?

package deals

COUCH: WITH A NAME LIKE THAT, he might sound like some kind of Potato, but that would be the wrong idea. He's the only kid I know who never watches TV—except for the movies we watch on Tuesday nights and The Sports Network, and he stretches and lifts weights while he watches the Network. His life is pretty much made up of:

- hockey (his number one thing)
- in-line skating (in the summer)
- lacrosse (because it's cheap)
- high diving (because it's scary)
- downhill skiing (same as above)
- BMX and
- freestyle biking (of course)!

When he was a little kid, he played football, but he gave that up when his dad decided to move here from Boston. Couch decided he didn't want to play Canadian rules. I guess it was tradition, his dad being a Ram and all.

Besides the football difference, he discovered something else when he came to Canada. He discovered that if you have a name like Chester Field, you're going to be called Couch.

In the States they don't have chesterfields—they have couches and sofas. His parents didn't know.

Couch and I go back a long way. Back to grade five when I had a cast on my leg and Amber, the school bully, ran off with my crutches. Then I didn't tower over people the way I do now. I was kind of short even. The sight of me with a broken leg was too much for Amber.

I remember Couch the first time I heard him. He was hollering at Amber and had wrestled one of the crutches from her hands. "You might need this soon yourself!"

She dropped the other crutch and ran down the hallway towards the principal's office. But she didn't report Couch. She knew better. Her reign was over.

I never did tell Couch why I had that cast on my leg. He guessed it was from a ski trip the class had gone on just before he moved into the neighbourhood, and I let him think that. Really, it happened when I was helping Mum get the Christmas lights out of the top shelf of the closet, and I lost my balance and fell off the stool.

I should've told him. It was one of those things that happens at the beginning of a friendship, when you don't know how important this person is going to be and a sort-of lie seems okay. Maybe it's still like that, and he sees me a little differently from how I really am. Then again, maybe not. I've always liked how he doesn't question a lot of stuff. Like, he's never asked about my father, and he doesn't question that that's something I just don't talk about. Maybe some people would think he's never asked because he doesn't care or he just hasn't thought to ask. But I don't think so.

Lately, things haven't been too good for Couch. Mr. Trevitt decided he couldn't play in the playoffs because Ms. Potter said his grades didn't cut it. The team was counting on him. They lost in the first round, and Couch lost a lot of guys he used to call friends.

"They aren't friends," I told him. "It's not your fault." Of course, it might have helped if he'd shown up in class once in awhile. Now he sees lots of Ms. Potter: Monday and Thursday after school for at least an hour.

I find Couch at our lockers. "You weren't in class."

"I see enough of Ms. P." He slams his locker door. "Why? Did I miss anything?"

"No. Only class," I can't resist saying, and feel a twinge of guilt over my own relief that he cut class.

Couch starts down the hall just as Ms. Potter steps out of the classroom.

He turns quickly, heads back towards me.

"Oh, Chester! I'd like to speak with you for a moment."

He grimaces, his lips move, and I know what he's muttering, but he does turn around.

"Ms. Potter," he says aloud.

Ms. Potter points to the door she's just come from. "Room 204," she says. She traces over the numbers on the door. "Or do you have as many problems with numbers as you do with letters? Let me introduce you: this is my English classroom. We would be honoured by your occasional presence, Mr. Field." Her voice carries down the hall.

Couch says nothing.

Ms. Potter moves slightly so that she can see me standing behind Couch. She points a long finger at me.

"Even Mr. Kidd is coming around," she says.

I see Couch's ponytail twitch as he turns around to look at me. His eyebrows are up.

Ms. Potter continues. "Yes—even Mr. Kidd is revealing a hidden talent for English."

Couch's lips hardly move. "What's she talking about?"

I shrug before I think.

Ms. Potter walks by both of us and pats me on the shoulder as she passes. Couch stares at my shoulder.

"What's she talking about?" His voice is higher.

"I dunno. You know how teachers are. I musta done my homework right or something."

"Yeah—teachers." Couch catches that part anyway. He waits until Ms. Potter rounds the far corner, then starts down the hall again, stops, says, "See you for T.C. tonight."

Mr. F makes the best tuna casserole. It has black olives and pimientos, curry and cayenne, and sometimes even crunched-up potato chips. He makes it for me on Tuesdays when Mum teaches upholstering at night school. In Grade Six, Couch and I decided we'd share our one dad.

"I'll be over right after I mow the grass."

Couch nods. He knows the deal I had to make with Mum: yard work in exchange for having the half-pipe.

"See you, Kidd."

Roland comes down the hall toward us. "Forgot your English text?" He spies Couch's book on top of the locker.

Roland means to be helpful—I've learned that much about him—but Couch walks over, opens his locker with one hand, shoves the book in, closes and locks the door.

Roland stares after him for a moment. "He's never going to be on the hockey team if he doesn't open a book once in awhile." He shakes his head. "But it's none of my business."

"Yeah. Don't worry about Couch," I tell him.

But Roland does. Worries about everyone. I don't know why really. Just like, I don't know why he made such a fuss about my poem.

"Couch doesn't worry about you," I add, and zip up my knapsack.

"No—he probably doesn't." Roland follows me out the door and down the wide steps. "Did you tell him about the poem?"

My answer is quick. "No."

Roland's eyes are like a slapshot. "Why not?"

"Couch isn't a poetry guy."

Roland raises a brow. "I guess you wish I'd never dared you."

I don't tell him he's right. I just say, "What's done is done," and watch as he walks away, his right shoulder sagging with the weight of his bookbag.

Some part of me sags too. For the second time now I've lied to Couch. Not lied exactly, but not told the truth either.

ROLAND IS AN ORIGINAL. His first day at school we all thought he was strange. Most of us still do. A bit anyway. There's something about that plain navy school tie he always wears. He has a few of them, all the same. "I really wanted to throw them out," he said. "That was going to be the best thing about public school—but I feel as if my head's going to fall off my neck when I don't have one on. I need my tie."

I can't say that any of us understand that, but he does wear a toque: olive green with a cuff. That we understand.

He's decent on a bike. Must be natural ability; his mother doesn't let him go near the public skate park. She probably doesn't even know he can ride as well as he does.

His parents make my mum look like a sports fan. Mum doesn't like my having a half-pipe, but at least she doesn't think that all freestylers are delinquents.

Roland's home is to the south of the delta, high on the cliff overlooking the ferry terminal. Once in awhile, he lets me know what's going on there, but I have to read between the lines. I get the feeling that someday he'll just take off. Of course it'll be in a civilized way—university or travel to Europe—but that'll be it. He'll be gone. Like his sister: she went to law school back east, and now she works in Toronto. She never even writes home. She just sends newspaper clippings of what she's doing, because what she's doing is usually in the paper. Roland's father puts the clippings away in a special file in his desk. I'll bet he takes out those clippings, shows them to Roland, and says, "See? This is what you can do when you graduate, son." Roland never tells me that part. He did tell me that his dad signed him up for certain classes next year—classes that Roland doesn't want to take. It's as if his parents don't know who he is.

Sometimes, when Roland thinks I'm not home or when I'm doing my homework, I hear him out in the yard. Once he offered to help me out with money for the extension and another platform, but I said no. I could just imagine what Couch would have to say. There's too many differences between those two already. I always feel stuck in the middle.

WE EAT T.C. IN OUR USUAL WAY: on the coffee table, pulled over our knees, our backs against the chesterfield, and Mr. F in his favourite chair. After, Couch and I wash dishes while his dad goes to the video store. Mr. F usually chooses some sports movie, or something funny. In winter he lights a fire and heats up apple cider. In the summer we throw a ball around the park beside their house and forget the movie entirely. In-between nights, like this one, we hang out in the glassed-in porch, and finish the T.C. with Mr. F's Amazing Oatmeal Cookies.

"Perfectly healthy for growing athletes," he says, carrying a plate with cookies tumbling over the edge. Pavel, Couch's golden lab, picks up the spills, and bits of oatmeal and raisins spew over the indoor-outdoor carpet.

"Gotta prepare for summer hockey school!" Mr. F hands us each a couple. "Yeah—summer school," Couch echoes, but his voice is flat and he gives me a funny look. A look like, "Don't say anything!"

Mr. F goes on. "Ms. Potter'll be finished with

you by then. Though you should keep up your reading for September."

"Yeah—keep up my reading." Couch nods.

"Athletes should be able to read more than a scoreboard." Mr. F laughs.

"But it's all so boring. Who needs it? I don't! Not to play hockey. Ms. P expects us to read novels and *poetry*. All this rhyming crap and...what does she call them? Couplets? Written by all these dead guys. Probably 'cause no one does that stuff anymore."

I wonder if Couch would notice if I just left now. On the other hand, we've been eating T.C. on Tuesday for four years, and this might be the last time. I should stay.

"Well," says Mr. F, putting his feet up, sitting back, "it'll all be over soon, and summer will be with us again." He touches the remote button and turns the video on.

He doesn't allow anyone to speak when the movie is on, so he presses the *pause* button if we want to talk about something, and then he starts the movie again. Once we finally saw the last scene of a show after midnight because of talking, and sometimes—and those are the best—sometimes we end up turning the movie off and just talking.

Couch's dad tells us stories about when he played football. Couch has heard them all before, many times. But I love to listen. And Mr. F loves to tell. I know by the look on his face when he pushes the rewind button on the VCR, turns the TV off, and settles into a story. They always begin with, "In the old days..." and Couch yawns, even closes his eyes, but he listens. He straightens his dad out on some detail he's forgotten or changed. I think his dad changes his stories just a little each time to see if Couch is listening.

"You sure you're going to be all right going home on that bike?" asks Mr. F, as the credits roll by. He asks that every week, and I nod yes. In the worst of winter he insists on putting my bike in the back of his truck and giving me a ride home.

Couch follows me down to the gate, and as I leave, he says: "Dad knows I had to miss the playoffs, but I haven't told him yet I have to do English in summer school and they might not let me on the team next year. If they even want me. Just because they want my hockey playing, doesn't mean they want me."

"Tell 'em you're a package deal."

"Ha! I like that: a package deal. You're a good guy, Kidd. Hey, I figure if I can get the English done in July, I can still do hockey camp in August. Have you signed up yet?"

"Maybe. I'll think about it."

"What's there to think about?"

He grins, then walks back to the house.

stubby pencil

THE PAPER COMES ON WEDNESDAY, and Wednesday is worse than I imagined.

Of course I hide the paper. It's just sitting there on the doorstep as I come home from school. I pick it up, amazed Mum hasn't gotten there first, and I stick it inside the camellia bush by the door.

I don't even peek inside—not that I don't want to, I admit—but I'm afraid Mum will have a sudden yen to poke her head out the door.

She doesn't look at me as I enter the kitchen. Which is a good sign. If she did, *then* I would know she knew something.

The kitchen is the largest room in our house. The house is old and we have the gas stove that was there when it was built. A big clunky thing with lots of chrome, like an old Chevy. The gas flames are a little scary. Once Mum lit a cigarette and scorched her eyebrows. That time I almost had her convinced to quit. Now I save matches for her and make sure I leave them in all her favourite light-up places. At least she hasn't used the stove since.

The stove takes up almost one entire wall of the room and one of the other walls is all windows— tall windows with little tiny panes that Mum gets me to wash in the spring and fall. Ninety-six of them. I counted the panes last time I washed them. I think that washing ninety-six panes of glass should be worth something in dollars and cents, but Mum doesn't see it that way. Instead, she makes me lemon meringue pie or stays up late to mend my knee-pads. They're always falling apart.

We have this table. Mum made it. She gave up trying to find one in a store or at an auction. It's the longest table I've ever seen. We eat at one end—at one corner of one end. And next to where we eat is Mum's upholstery sewing machine. The machine is always in the way of my elbow—that's the problem with being left-handed. I tried to talk Mum into letting me sit at the end of the table, but she says that's her place.

Next to the sewing machine is the cutting area—where she cuts the heavy cloth, and there's always bits of threads and straggles of cloth under the table on the floor. Then there's her drawing table, usually with a mound of papers. When she does work at the drawing table, it's late at night. All I ever see her do there is read the newspaper, standing up with coffee or scissors or a cigarette in her hand.

"Did you see the paper as you came in?" she asks around a mouthful of pins.

When I was little I thought she'd swallow them accidently some day, but she never has.

"No," I lie. Sometimes I'm surprised how easy it is to lie if you do it quickly.

She looks at her watch, gives it a sharp tap with her finger, looks at it again. "Always broken." At least she doesn't throw it this time. She puts the last pin in the thick velvet stuff. "Maybe it wasn't delivered. I'll just phone them." Her hand reaches for the phone. "I'm running out of pieces to work on. I have to do some serious garage sale-ing this week."

Before I can think further, I say: "Maybe I'll just check again. Maybe I missed it." I go out the door. I don't want some kid to get in trouble big-time for a paper he did deliver. So I rummage in the camellia bush. There it is. Page 4. Wow—pretty close to the front, isn't it? I'm about to rip it out, but I check...Page 4 connects with page 13. Uh huh. The garage sales and the "free" columns are on page 13. If I take that page out, Mum will notice! No chance of ripping it in half either. She'll definitely notice.

Then one of those rare things happens. A true brainwave. A real thought. *"Spill something on it."* Even Roland didn't think of that.

I take the paper inside the house. Slowly. Slowly, so I can plot. Ah, yes. There's Mum's coffee. If I set the paper down on the table—the one bare spot, my place—casually turn to page 4, and then oops! Gee, I'm sorry, Mum. Here, let me. I'll be happy to make you a fresh pot. You've no idea how happy. Take time from my homework to make you, my mum, fresh coffee? No problem.

That'll work. It's got to.

There it is—the coffee. But it's not anywhere near the bare spot on the table. It's at Mum's elbow, of course. I should have known. I can't put the paper on top of her work, then casually flip pages.

I pass by the table. Peer into her mug. There's barely a mouthful left. Hardly enough to do damage.

21

"Well?" Mum asks. "Are you going to stand there all day with the paper tucked underneath your arm?"

I throw it onto the table, where it sort of *plops*. I don't mean to throw it. I think I really wanted to run back out the door with it, but my arm begins to swing before I can stop it, and then my fingers open just as my arm reaches its highest point. So it plops, and a camellia leaf falls out of the folded pages.

Now that it's done, I want it over with. But no. Mum turns the entire paper over, and opens it as always—from the back—to page 13. Then she walks slowly to the pen holder by her drawing board and rummages around for her red marker, ambles back to her seat, sits down, lights a cigarette, and goes through the "free" column. She sighs, then begins slowly marking the "garage sale" column. This will take time.

Here goes. One final attempt.

"Umm?...Mum...why don't I just rip that page off for you and I can read the rest?"

She looks up at me and speaks slowly. "Rip the page?"

"Not a good idea, huh?"

She lowers her head, writes a big number one next to an item, then a number two.

Well, I tried.

I cover the one bare spot on the table with my math text and pretend to study.

Finally she's finished with page 13. Flip, goes the page. I can almost feel a little gust of air from the turning paper. Another, then another. I try not to count them.

Then she's there.

There's a big photo—not of me, of course—but of someone, some freestyler, flying off one end of a half-pipe. So she sniffs, which is her usual re-action to anything athletic.

Then she leans over. "There's an article or something about freestyling...." Her voice drifts off.

OR SOMETHING, I want to yell.

"What is this?" she asks, very quietly.

"It's an Or-Something."

"It's a poem." She wiggles in her seat and sits up straighter, which is not good. This is her "read-aloud" position.

> "Freestyling"
> by Ogilvie Kidd.

She looks at me. I look at my math book. She begins again.

> "Freestyling"
> by Ogilvie Kidd.

> *wheels spin*
> *air all around me*
> *and under*
> *I'm off the top*
> *my body turns against the sun*
> *as gravity laughs and reels me in*
> *I pass the summit*
> *and drop*
> *feet*
> *knees*
> *stomach*
> *thud*

> *pedals move   rush*
> *rubber hums buzz over wood*
> *push up   up   up*
> *air born.*

Then there's this silence. And I'm not a writer, and I'm not a poet, so I can't describe it, except to say that it seemed long. Long like when you're in the air and you know you're going to crash. And you wish you could enjoy the flight, the freedom of being not quite human for that split second, but you're too worried about how hard the ground is going to be.

Mum reads the poem again. And again, mumbling. Then silently.

She starts to cry. "I wish your grandpa was alive."

"Mum?"

She wipes her tears. "I mean, I would like for you to know him, and I would like for him to know you." She rattles the paper in her hand. "He'd be so proud of you. Another poet in the family."

I have to think of something to comfort her. Something that is absolutely perfect and calms her tears.

Mum keeps a photo of Grandpa on one of the bricks jutting out of the chimney behind the old stove. So I take it down and place it on the table between us.

"You've told me so much about Grandpa that I feel I do know him, Mum."

"You do?" Mum looks at me with upraised brows and holds her cigarette in the air above her shoulder. I don't think she believes me, but she'd really like to. I'd like to too.

I turn the photo so I'm looking directly at him. I've seen this picture so many times. There he is, in his loose jacket, heavy corduroy trousers, and his pipe. Always that pipe. My only other picture of him is the one I carry in my mind. The one that was put there by Mum telling me about Grandpa writing poetry. He's sitting at a big roll-top desk with his head bent over a pile of papers and he's scribbling furiously. He pauses, stares out the window, and begins to scribble furiously again. He's writing about the sunset and the moon and the length of winter. This is the picture I always see when I think of Grandpa the Poet. Now that picture flashes into my mind and to my horror I realize he's writing with a quill pen! He has this enormous, old-fashioned, white feather pen in his hand! It's so obvious, I wonder how I never saw it before. Where did it come from? How long has it been in the picture?

"Did Grandpa write with a quill pen?"

Mum's shocked. "Of course not. He wasn't around that long ago. He usually used a stubby carpenter's pencil."

A stubby carpenter's pencil? The picture I've had of Grandpa suddenly becomes a puzzle and breaks into a hundred pieces.

I THOUGHT WEDNESDAY WAS BAD.

When I wake up on Thursday, my first thought is of Couch, and I wonder if he's seen the poem. Everyone in town gets the paper.

I pull on my jeans and open my top drawer where I've been saving the new shirt Mum bought for my birthday. Almost two months ago, but I save things. Not for anything in particular. Maybe just because Mum hardly ever buys anything new.

This shirt is wild. The pattern looks like pea green seagulls flying between purple stripes. Mum thought it might be good for job interviews in the summer.

I think it'll be good for today. I put it on. And take it off.

Today I'll wear my corduroy shirt, the one Couch borrows when he stays over, the one he's always hassling me for. And I find my Canucks cap under the novel for English class. I put the cap on and take the book downstairs.

Downstairs at the table, Mum waits. For once, almost half the table is clear, and there are two places actually set for breakfast. Mum likes to work in the morning. Often she's still up from the night before and just about to finish something, and too excited to eat.

But this morning, she's going to eat with me.

I see that she has taped the entire page four of the newspaper to the fridge and circled the poem with red felt pen.

"I'm going to *The Optimist* for more copies," she says as she notices me looking at the fridge.

Why can't she just have a file in a drawer like Roland's father has? In Roland's kitchen, the fridge is big and white. And clean. His mum's probably never taped anything onto it.

Lying across my plate, there's a book. I pick it up and feel the purple velvet cover. If it had a title, it's long worn off. Now there's just silver flecks here and there.

Mum stands beside me, hugging a cereal box close, watching.

I open the book. *Malcolm Kidd*, my grandfather's name, is in the front cover. I turn the page.

Behold the spring and the bird's nest....

Oh no.

"Beautiful, isn't it?" Mum's eyes are shiny.

I put the book beside my plate. "What's for breakfast?"

"Don't you like it?"

"I don't know—what is it?"

"*Poems of Season.* It was your grandfather's."

"Mum—I'm really hungry. And I have to be at school soon."

"School," Mum says, and her eyes suddenly focus on me. "I've been meaning to show you this." She flies to the far end of the table and rummages through one of the piles. Amazing how she always knows where everything is.

"This!" She puts a piece of paper on my plate, and I have barely enough time to see a photo of an old stone building, and the name Burr Lake Academy, before she whisks it away and reads it aloud herself.

" 'Burr Lake Academy is accepting applications for scholarships. Two young men will receive full tuition as well as room and board....' "

"A *boarding* school?" Okay, so my voice can still go a little high now and then.

"It's a wonderful school. We can send a copy of your poem with your application. Now that you're a published poet, you stand a better chance...."

"Mum!"

She stops, her mouth still open.

"I can't leave here." I can't leave my friends, my half-pipe. Guaranteed, they don't have a half-pipe at that place, Burr Lake.

I think of Roland and that tie around his neck. His old school was St. Albert's. His parents took him there when he was so young he didn't know what to think of it. But I know what I think: I do not want to go to a place called *Academy*.

Mum finally sits down to eat. She sips her coffee. "You can come home for holidays and every weekend, you know. It wouldn't be that bad. I could get used to it." That's what she says, though she does bury her face in her cup again, quickly.

"You could?"

"I could," she says. "This could open such wonderful opportunities for you, Ogilvie. Opportunities I never had."

"Mum," I interrupt her. "Take the opportunity to eat your breakfast. It's not good to start the day on an empty stomach." I imitate her, and she laughs like I've said something really funny.

She goes on. "Just last night I noticed in the paper a list of summer programs, and they're offering an arts camp...here." She pulls out the paper from under another pile and reads aloud.

> *Watch for:*
> *Summer programs, details TBA*
> *Vegetarian Barbecuing*
> *Beach Fun for Tots*
> *Arts Camp for Teens*

"Mum." I pick up my English book, grab my jacket from the wall by the door. "I gotta go. I'm going to be late."

MALLORY'S AT THE SCHOOL GATE as if she's waiting for me or something. When she sees me, she sort of skips forward. "Og," she says.

I look over and see Roland sitting, one leg on either side of the wide stone stair railing leading to the front door of the school, and Couch leaning against the wall.

"Great poem, Og!" says Mallory, all in a rush.

"Thanks." I keep walking.

She follows me to the door. Couch's eyes are on her.

I hear somebody yell. "Hey! It's the Poet Genius!" I don't turn around.

I try to be cool, wave my hands, look at Roland. "This was your idea!"

"It was your genius!" Roland won't take any credit, not a word, not a footnote.

Couch still looks at Mallory, but he talks to me. "Great poem, Og!" He echoes Mallory, and for a really short minute, I think he might be serious.

Roland isn't fooled. He says, "I like the poem, Couch," and he scratches an eyebrow.

Couch squints at him. "You would. At least you *knew* about it!"

Roland says, "Relax, Couch. It's not like it was a big secret or something."

"No? Then how come nobody told me about it? Must've been a big secret."

"It was announced in class," I say. "Maybe if you came once in awhile...."

Couch goes on, talking to Roland as if I'm not even there. "Besides, Og shouldn't be writing poetry."

"Why not?" Roland is pulling at his brows; he's going to be one of those old guys with tufty wing-brows.

"'Cause he's not dead!"

"You don't have to be dead to write poetry," says Roland. "I think it's easier if you're somewhat alive."

"Tony Jones doesn't write poetry." Couch's voice is getting loud.

"How do *you* know what Tony Jones does? Just because you expect him to act a certain way, doesn't mean he has to. He could surprise you, you know," says Roland. His voice rises, too. "How do you know what *anyone* does?" He rattles the handle on his blue lunchbox and pulls his leg over the stone railing as the bell buzzes.

"I know Tony Jones wouldn't do something like write a poem," Couch mutters. "He's too busy working on his back flip." Couch's hands ramble around his jaw. Mr. F always says, "Keep your hands off your face and your skin'll clear up," but Couch forgets sometimes. Now he looks at me and goes on.

"Ms. P might have to raise your mark to C-minus for your end-of-term effort. Maybe you can study litter-ature, and be a professor...." He speaks in falsetto. "Do be careful, Professor. Don't get your lovely gown caught in the chain of your bicycle!"

Mallory starts moving toward the door.

"Mallory!" I call out after her. Geez, I wish Couch wouldn't go on like this.

I speak before I think. "Shut up, Couch."

But Couch has already—about Ms. Potter and poetry, anyway—and he's staring after Mallory. "I guess she likes you, doesn't she? Or maybe she likes the poem thing." He shoulders himself away from the wall and through the door.

Roland pushes me through the door and, as he does, he passes me a rolled-up copy of yesterday's paper.

I shove it back towards him. "I've seen enough of this!"

"Bet you didn't have time to look at page 10!"

He's right. On my desk I open the paper. There's the usual picture of the local ball team, the Tigers.

Then I see it—the photo in the lower right corner. "WATCH," the ad says. "THE DUDE HIMSELF IS COMING FOR YOU TO SEE. SOON."

Soon? No date. Just *soon*. Tony Jones. The best. Wow.

I look at Couch, across the aisle. Has he seen this? I roll the paper tightly and reach across the aisle and nudge his shoulder. He twitches, and then slams his math book onto the top of his desk. And on top of that, every book and all those papers he keeps in his bag. That stack usually means he hasn't done his English homework, and he uses it like a trench to hide in and fire at Ms. Potter.

"Couch!"

His head ducks lower. Just his ponytail shows. Sun-bleached already from spring skiing, and tied with a black elastic.

Damn that poem!

I pass the newspaper back to Roland just as Ms. Potter enters the room. She notices Couch first. "Mr. Field!" she says. "Welcome to room 204!" Then she looks at me.

"Ogilvie, you brought a copy of the paper. I'm so glad. Are you going to read for us?" She smiles this smile that could feed the world and stands between me and Couch, with her back to him.

I look at Roland. If *he'd* only grabbed it with a little more speed. He's smiling and nodding. I look at Couch, still buried. His elbow's moving. He must be scribbling on his paper. If he'd taken the newspaper, Ms. Potter wouldn't have noticed at all!

Ms. Potter sits on her desk, motions to the front. "Do read, Ogilvie."

Couch's eyes appear over the books, like a crocodile's above water, and his elbow stops moving for a minute.

Mallory's smiling too, nodding in time with Roland. Maybe it's easier to walk to the front of the class because it's Mallory in front of me and not Couch. But I have to face Couch when I'm up there. I feel his stare, and I can hear his pencil scratching at his paper as I read. (He never takes the time to sharpen them properly.) Mallory's still smiling, looking proud—so I look at her.

I read, and finish:

> *push up   up   up*
> *air born*

Then I walk back to my seat. I'm almost there and Couch's arm shoots across my path. There's his paper, and me on the paper: a drawing of me, except that I'm kind of bald and I have a clown collar around my neck and a clown nose. Underneath, Couch has printed SHAKESPEARE KIDD. And he's grinning.

He calls his drawings *tattoo plans*.

"Which arm are you gonna put that on?" I ask, as he slides it into the desk.

There are papers in every desk of every class Couch has. People in the next class usually pull them out, pass them around. The faces in the tattoo plans are always easy to recognize. Too easy. He didn't need to put my name on. But he did. By afternoon, I'll be known as Shakespeare Kidd.

When I leave class, Ms. Potter smiles at me. She's never smiled at me before. She doesn't say anything about *Freestyling*, though.

If I think about it—really think about it—try to remember if her teeth showed, or if the left side of her mouth was a little higher than the right, or just how was it that she smiled—maybe she didn't smile at me at all. Maybe she was just looking out the window as teachers do, and maybe she saw a bit of blue between the clouds, or a cat spring to miss a car in the street.

COUCH IS LIKE CLOCKWORK about some things—like the half-pipe on Saturdays. Usually I'm just spooning in the last bite of Mum's cracked wheat cereal and there he is, hammering at the screen door. He always asks the same question: "Why do you lock that thing when you know I'm coming?"

And my answer: "Because it's so early I forget to unlock it." It's tradition.

Then he fills a bowl with cracked wheat—there's always a supply in the fridge—pours milk on it, sticks it in the microwave and paces back and forth in front of the sink while the oven whirrs. Ding! and he pushes some of Mum's scraps and pattern pieces out of his way, sits down opposite me, and eats—even though I know he just polished off a bowl of granola and maybe some Saturday morning pancakes at home with his dad.

He complains about the cracked wheat cereal. That's tradition too. "Slimy stuff," he calls it. But never in front of Mum.

Mum scares him. I could be wrong about that—Couch is very careful not to give himself away—but I do think Mum scares him.

Couch's folks have been divorced forever. His mum's back in the States somewhere. She's always moving. Last place I remember is Tucson, but that was a while ago. Couch sees her every couple of years or so, when she writes and says she's ready for him. Every time, he says, "This is it, I'm not gonna go." He always goes though.

When we were kids, Couch used to want to find a woman for his dad to marry. I remember when he found out Mum was single. "My dad's gotta meet your mum...blah, blah, blah."

Then they met when Mum picked me up at the arena and the four of us went for a hot dog. Couch never said anything about it again. I think it had something to do with Mum wearing two different socks, her favourite patched longjohns, and a sweater stretched to her knees. And Mr. F's a health freak, so her cigarettes no doubt finished it off.

"So...he's an old professional football player, eh?" That's all Mum said as we drove away from the hot dog place that day.

But Couch is late today. Maybe he's not coming at all.

When I phone, Mr. F's long message rambles on. Nobody's home.

Mum slams through the kitchen door from an early round of garage-sailing. "You're not on your bike yet! Good—come with me to the lumberyard. You can help me find some moulding."

I like the lumberyard, the smell of raw cedar. I like to look at the plywood, the great stacks of two-by-fours, and imagine my half-pipe with an extension.

AT THE LUMBERYARD I realize what Mum wants the moulding for: a frame. For my poem.

"What do you think? Is this the right size?" She holds up her hands, her thumbs sticking out, and she makes a square of about thirty centimeters.

"Where are you going to put this?" I ask.

Mum's checking out different widths of fancy mouldings, bending her head at her thinking angle.

"In the hall," she says absent-mindedly.

"It'd look real nice upstairs," I suggest.

She's not paying attention.

"Upstairs!" I whisper loudly as I pass behind her. I wander up the aisles, looking at tools and saws and things I don't know the names of.

There's an aisle with tape measures that SNAP when they roll up, and screwdrivers with lots of bits—flat bits and Robertson bits and Phillips bits, and pencils. Flat, wide carpenter's pencils, in red and grey. It'd take a long time for one of these to become stubby. A lot of poetry, I think. I pick one up. It feels strange in my hand, but I like the flatness. Reminds me of skipping rocks.

After I pay for the pencil and put it in my pocket, I go to the plywood section. I guess I'm hoping the price'll go down, but it never does. My half-pipe's too narrow, and with only one platform above the ground, it's quite dangerous, though I never mention that in front of Mum. But I need a lot of wood. The two pieces from Roland will help, and so will my prize money, but it's not enough.

Mum's finished. She finds me because she knows I always end up here when we come to the lumberyard.

She rubs my head, which I hate—especially now that I'm taller than she is—and says, "Come on, my poet! Let's go home." She grabs my hand and pulls me away, like she did when I was little and looking for too long at the train through the toy store window.

I feel the flat pencil in my pocket. I think I'll tuck it behind the photo of Grandpa. I've read about people in other parts of the world who leave bowls of rice in front of pictures of their dead relatives, and somehow it seems right to leave a pencil with Grandpa's picture.

Mum's all excited when we get home—gets out her mitre box and saws away at the moulding. When the angles are just so, she fits it together. A little glue, BANG, BANG, a little paint or varnish, and there it is.

There's no rain today—a perfect day for the bike. Still no sign of Couch. I put on my pads and helmet and grab a sandwich.

I always start slow. Feel my bike, my real bike, not the Tin-Speed. This bike is chrome-plated, with alloy 48-spoked wheels. I've forfeited birthday and Christmas presents for two years because of this bike, and I've done a lot of neighbourhood yard work.

I pedal in lazy circles, around and around. The seat's squeaking a bit today—like it was last week—and the rear wheel could use a touch of air. I drift forward up the ramp and let the bike run backwards down, up again, down. It's always like this. Suddenly I get the feel of it, and I circle around, pedalling faster, up, up, faster, and then I get some air. I have to work on my can-cans. It's tough letting go and putting my leg right out there. There's always the urge to just hang on. But I do it: ride past the transition—the quarter turn—up over the coping— the edge—into the air, pull both legs over one side, then quickly back into place before I hit the plywood and ride down.

Then I crash, as I do every so often. It's part of it, I tell Mum, but for a brief minute I forget that crashing is part of it. Like now. On a perfect Saturday, after a perfect can-can, I crash. And I feel cactus-red heat in my left knee.

I sit on the plywood, holding my knee, hoping Mum hasn't heard me—the crash or my yell—and it happens. Just like when I wrote that poem. Suddenly words pop into my head. Words like *cactus-red heat, teeth grit.*

Then the urge is gone but the pain is still there. I close my eyes and rest my head on my knee and suddenly I wonder about Grandpa. Did this happen to him? These words banging against the insides of his ears? I even picture them to be something like a bike on a half-pipe—furiously moving from one side to the other, back and forth, faster and faster.

The wheel on my bike is still spinning. I reach out and clamp my hand around the thick rubber squares of tread and it stops. My thumb hurts; I must have rolled over it.

Couch pushes his bike through the space in the hedge, catches me shaking the pain from my hand.

"Hurt your writin' fingers?" He doesn't wait for me to answer. "Where'd you go this morning? Why'd you jam out? I thought Saturday was our regular thing. It's like missing T.C."

"You were late. And Mum needed my help."

"Maybe you could wait a few minutes. Or was Ms. Mallory in a rush?"

"What are you talkin' about? I just said my mum needed help."

Couch is riding backwards and forwards, as slowly as he can. "You know what I'm talkin' about."

"Couch—*what* are you talkin' about?"

"Nothing."

"I did phone you. You weren't home."

"I was on my way."

"That was over an hour ago."

"Let's just forget it." He sounds angry and he speeds up. I can hardly hear his words over the hum of his tires.

Then he stops, and I ask, "What was that about Mallory?"

He stares at me for a minute. "Mallory...." he starts. Then stops.

I say, "I'm sorry I didn't wait longer for you. I miss one morning. It doesn't have to be such a big deal...."

I'm not even finished speaking and he's disappeared through the hedge.

I call after him. "What *about* Mallory?"

opportunities

OF COURSE MUM PUTS THE POEM in the entrance hall. Next to the photo of three-month-old me looking at that picture book. She's still hammering away and fitting bits of moulding.

But she hears me come in, hears my silence as I stand in the hall, and she comes to meet me.

"What do you think?" she motions to the wall.

"All right."

"I've decided that this is going to be the family art gallery," she says.

A photograph of me reading a book is hardly art.

"I'm going to frame a poem of your grandpa's, and put it right here." She touches a faded square on the old wallpaper. "And one of your grandmother's drawings."

I say, "Mum, what about all the wonderful artwork of my childhood? That should be on these walls. What would you call them? Those..." words do a half-pipe in my mind again. "Those EMBRYONIC art pieces. Those WORKS that revealed my potential at such a young age...."

Ah! I've struck a sore point. My mum's ideas of an artistic child. I was never allowed to have a

COLOURING BOOK. Mum always said she didn't want me to be restricted. So I had giant rolls of brown wrapping paper, and the back sides of wallpaper, and I was supposed to feel FREE with my wax crayons—always boxes of 64! The biggest you could get back then.

All that paper scared the crap out of me!

Finally I began to draw tiny stickmen in the corners, or near the edges of the paper. Then I drew stickmen with hockey sticks and pucks and stickmen with skis and stickmen with bicycles. That was my childhood artwork. Stickmen at sports. Underfed jocks.

Mum is standing really straight. "Ogilvie," she says, "if it's the last thing I do, I'm going to make sure you have the opportunities that I didn't have."

Uh-oh.

SCHOOL ON MONDAY. There's a cheque waiting for me in the office, from *The Optimist*. My winnings. Twenty bucks and a gift certificate for BONNIE'S BOOKS, the only bookstore in town. I'll give the certificate to Mum. She likes the bookstore. Maybe I can get the cheque without a chat from the principal. He tends to do that as soon as I'm in his office.

Mr. Trevitt hands the envelope to me and looks proud.

"Guess you're not always on that bike of yours, young man," he says.

Three times he's caught me and Couch leaving tread marks in the gym and doing 360s over the curbs out front.

"Think you'll exchange the wheels for a pen now?" He sits on the front of his desk, one foot on the floor, the other swinging from a bent knee. I know this position. The Position for Conversation.

"Don't think so," I say, and quickly add, "sir." Maybe if I'm polite he won't go on. I move toward the door. Now my hand's on the knob. Turning.

He opens his mouth to say something.

I pull. Wave the cheque. "Bye. Sir. Thanks."

Click.

The office door closes behind me. The hallway is empty because first class has begun and my footsteps echo.

Why does it have to be one thing or the other? I can be either a freestyle-bike freak, OR a pen-handling poet. But not both.

Suddenly I'm angry because I liked the feeling of that flat pencil in my hand. Okay, not as much as I like the feel of my feet on the pedals, or getting air on the half-pipe, but I did like it.

Twenty bucks. That'll help with the plywood.

COUCH POINTS TO HIS WATCH and looks approving as I slide into my desk late.

Ms. Potter frowns, then raises her brows.

I wave the cheque. "Just picking up my winnings."

Her brows are still raised, as if she's forgotten.

"For the poem," I remind her.

The brows come down.

"How much?" asks Couch.

I look at the cheque casually. "Twenty bucks."

"What are you going to do with twenty bucks?" He leans forward for my answer.

"Think I'll pick up some wood for the half-pipe."

Couch nods, and I feel as if I've passed some sort of test.

I wonder: how many more tests is he going to put me through? How many more Saturdays will he be late, and then freak out on me later? I stare at his profile.

Hey, Couch. What's with you, man?

"YOU GONNA COME FOR T.C. TONIGHT?"

Couch never asks me for T.C. Usually, he just mentions it—something like "See you at six," or "Dad's gonna be late tonight, and wants us to boil the macaroni." But today he actually asks.

I never miss it. "Why wouldn't I?"

He shrugs.

MUM HAS TO GO EARLY TO TEACH. "I'll ride with you," she says, and hauls her tricycle out of the garage.

We pass the house where Mallory lives. At least, I think it's the house. Couch pointed it out to me a couple of years ago. It's in his neighbourhood.

"Whose house is that you're looking at?" asks Mum.

"Just somebody in my class."

"Hmm," she says, and she does the slow sideways look, with a little smirk.

We round the corner and there's Couch's place.

Mum stops in front. "What does Mr. Field think of your poem?"

That's something I haven't thought of.

Mum's shoulders straighten. "I know I'm proud of you. What does Couch think of Burr Lake?"

"I haven't told him."

"Oh," she says.

And I haven't told you about hockey camp, I add to myself.

"Well, bye-bye." She waves and puts her hands to the handlegrips and goes, a bolt of fabric and several yardsticks poking out from the big basket in back.

Before I can head home—that's what I suddenly feel like doing—Pavel comes careering down the driveway, barking, and the screen door opens. Mr. F yells, "Come in—you're just in time!"

Couch is pulling the casserole out of the oven with big mitts on his hands. There's a stack of three plates on the coffee table, and I start to spread them out, just as the phone rings.

"Yep," I hear Mr. F say. Then, "I'll have to phone you tomorrow, Wolfgang. I'm just sitting to dinner with my boys here....That's right. I have one son, but on Tuesday nights, I have two." He laughs, looks at me. "I'll see you at work tomorrow. Talk with you then." He hangs up, grabs cutlery from the drawer.

Couch is pretty quiet while we eat, but Mr. F talks and doesn't notice. He talks about the past week at work. Four people have been laid off, and now the other employees are too busy. He talks on, between mouthfuls, and I begin to think that maybe he missed last week's paper. Almost at the end of the T.C...and he says, "So that poem of yours—that's fine stuff."

Am I supposed to say thanks?

Mr. F reaches for the remote. It's movie time. But he isn't quite finished. "I could become a fan of sports poetry, Ogilvie. Good for you!" Even as Mr. F speaks, Couch leaps from his chair.

"Where're you going?" asks his dad.

"Wash dishes," Couch mumbles from in the kitchen.

Mr. F gives me a puzzled look.

Okay. Can I go home now?

WEDNESDAY WHEN I GET HOME after school the newspaper's on the front step just like it was last week.

I hand it to Mum. "Roland and I are riding," I tell her, and we go out to the yard.

We warm up together, two seagulls circling lazily, then dipping, then I hang to the side as Roland works on his no-footed airs. He's been working on those for a long time. If he'd just do it—take his feet off the pedals, fly them out to the sides—he'd be fine. But he leaves the coping, gets into the air, starts to put his feet out...then pulls back. Seems as if the more he works on it, the worse it gets. Maybe he's scared. Scared of what? He does other tricks that are equally hard. "Come on, Roland," I urge, then wish I hadn't. His face folds and his eyes go dark. I shouldn't have said anything. I probably sound like his mum.

Still, I'm wishing that cheque was a lot bigger—big enough to buy an extension, so we could both ride at the same time, when Mum comes flying out the door.

Mum's like a cat when she's angry—especially

when she's defensive. Her back sort of rounds up, and the hair at the top of her head seems to stand up like the hair in an old sixties movie. What did they call it? Backcombed.

Here she is, flying out the door. Waving the newspaper.

"If you can stop riding those bicycles in circles, I'll read this to you. Someone wrote a letter to the editor about your poem!"

"Hey, that's good!" says Roland.

Mum almost hisses. "No it's not!"

Something tells me, I don't want to hear this letter.

Dear Editor,
  I am writing in response to your paper's prize-winning display of solidarity with what I will call the Ruffian Element in our society....

Roland's frowning. "Who's he calling a ruffian?" he asks.

"You," Mum says. "You are a ruffian." She snaps the paper, looks at the letter she's reading. "You are a ruffian according to one Mr. Britt. Or at least Ogilvie is, and you are his friend, so no doubt you are too." She snaps the paper again and glares at us. "Let me continue."

I wish her hair would go down a bit.

She starts again:

  Your publication of a piece of written work—I refuse to call such a display a "poem"—which condones the use of those

dreadful machines known as BMX bi-
cycles, is horrendous. I expect so much
more from The Optimist. *Of course, one*
cannot expect a newspaper to encourage
literature in our children, but surely the
nature of a POETRY contest ought to
have been POETRY. This minimalist
physical-sensations-of-athletics thing
can hardly be described as POETRY.

WHAT are they teaching children
at the schools these days if they think
THIS is POETRY?

POETRY is about beauty and love.
What does a fifteen-year-old boy know
about that?

Roland snorts and stands up over his bike, picks
up the handlebars and drops the front wheel, keeping the bike between his legs as the tire bounces.
He's anxious to be moving again. Enough of Mr.
Britt.

I think, Enough of Mr. Britt too, but for different reasons. For one thing, I don't like to think
that anyone actually read my poem and cared
enough to be angry about it—I have enough of that
with Couch! Besides, I hate to say it, but I kind of
agree with him. Poetry is about love and beauty.
Mr. Britt is probably close to the age Grandpa was
when he wrote poetry. He should know.

And suddenly I have this terrible feeling. What
if Grandpa was like Mr. Britt? After all, I really
know nothing at all about my grandfather. Would
he be horrified, just like this Mr. Britt, to discover
what his grandson has done to the Art of Poetry?

"I'll read the rest later, Mum," I yell loudly as I turn my back to her and pedal.

I can hear her muttering behind me, reading the letter to herself, and then she goes in the house.

Roland watches me, but I do tricks in the left-handed direction and it's hard to follow what I'm doing, so he gives up and just rides.

"Is Couch coming over?" he asks.

"I don't know—he didn't say anything."

"Did you ask him?"

"Ask him? He's usually just here."

"But he's acting kinda strange lately—even for Couch," says Roland. "Maybe you should ask him." He crashes.

"It's the poetry thing, I think."

"Who knows?" He rights his bike. "He seems to think it was some big secret we had."

"Why can't he just forget it?" I say.

"Maybe he thinks you're changing."

"How?"

"I think he's always seen you as a half-pipe freak who's right up there near the top."

This is quite flattering.

"Well?" I ask. "How have I changed? I write one lousy poem. That doesn't mean anything."

Roland doesn't answer.

"It won't last," I say. How can it? There are only two half-pipes in town and even though mine's only half finished, it's better than the one in the park, and it's better than nothing. Besides, Couch and his dad helped me build this one. He's got to get over it.

I wish he'd just forget this poetry thing. I wish everyone would: Mum, with her frame-making and

48

Burr Lake Academy and arts camp, and Roland and Mr. Britt and...everyone.

IT'S ABOUT THREE IN THE MORNING when I wake up, and it's really dark. There's no moon and the cedar hedge that surrounds most of the house hides almost all the street lights except for the one at the side yard, and it's burned out. I like it dark like this. This is when I know that this is my home. I know every wrinkle in the narrow, colour-lost runner that covers the hardwood of the hallway. I know the squeaks of the stairs. I know the bumpy moulding that crosses the floor and separates the entrance-way from the living room, and I know the gentle smell of Mum's smoke that tells me when she's awake. Tonight she's not. I can have the kitchen to myself.

I switch on the cone-shaped light Mum uses for sewing at night and pull the newspaper from the middle of the table into the small circle of warm light.

I read Mr. Britt's letter slowly. I read the last sentence again. "What does a fifteen-year-old boy know about beauty and love?"

What do I know? I look up from the paper and I see Mum's latest piece of work: a Mad Hatter chair, overstuffed, with bright sausages of red and gold and green fanned across the back. It'll take over someone's living room, belching colour and whimsy. That's beautiful.

Hawks are beautiful. At least they are until you see one ripping some small animal to pieces, and even that's kind of beautiful, in a wild, crimson way.

Maybe I know a bit about beauty.

Love. I love my mum, even when she drives me crazy. Even when she hangs that stupid thing on the wall. That's love.

But I think Mr. B means the romantic kind.

There's Lauren Gray. I've had a crush on her since Grade Eight—or at least I sweat every time I see her.

Something tells me that Mr. B probably wouldn't count that. So...what do I know about anything?

"Goodnight, Mr. Britt," I say as I fold the paper, shove it back to the centre of the table, and click the cone light off.

Then a whiff of smoke and I turn and see the glow of Mum's cigarette in the darkness at the doorway.

"You could write an answer, you know," she says.

"What would I say?"

Mum doesn't say anything. The ember glows brighter, then darkens as she exhales.

"You know, he might be right," I say.

"He might be wrong," she says. "I think poetry's a funny thing. It can answer questions or ask them. Sometimes it's for fun, and sometimes it's for remembering." She changes the subject. "Did you see Grandpa's poem that I hung in the hallway?"

I shake my head, which of course Mum can't see in the dark. She must think I'm not answering and she leaves after saying goodnight quietly.

I turn the light back on and search under newspapers and bits of fabric for a pen and writing paper.

What can I say to Mr. B?

"Poetry," said Ms. Potter, "poetry is the blood of all writing. It is the heart, the soul. It is the 'red, red rose.'"

I remember her saying that. It was just last fall when we were working on the poetry segment of Grade Ten English.

And then she read all this stuff—Sunset stuff. Flowers and rainbows and crap like that. Rhymes and sing-song. I fell asleep and Couch woke me up with a paper ball and a grin.

I'll bet Mr. B knows every one of those poems that Ms. Potter read us.

The paper in front of me is still blank.

When I hear one bird tweet, I turn the light off and see that there is a bit of a glow behind the cedar hedge.

I pass through the hall on my way upstairs and I almost stop, almost turn on the overhead light, almost read Grandpa's poem, but I don't.

Maybe tomorrow. I'm afraid Grandpa will be just like Mr B. And I don't want him to be.

I PASS GRANDPA'S POEM on the way out the door to school. I see out of the corner of my eye a new frame, bright red, next to mine, but I don't stop. I'd like to, but I can't. Yet.

First class is English, and there's Mallory, looking at me with those enormous moss-coloured eyes.

This is really stupid. I'm the bike-freak and she's...well, this is her favourite class.

I wonder if Grandpa wrote poems about girls. Poems about Grandma. I do remember Grandma.

Always sketching with her pad and charcoals. I remember accidently splashing her paper at the beach when she was sitting cross-legged in the shallow water and I was doing what kids always do at the beach. She wasn't upset. Instead she worked over her drawing for awhile, moving the salt-water drops, smudging with her fingertips, adding charcoal, holding the paper up to catch the light of the late summer afternoon. She was quite pleased with it after all that and said I could splash her artwork any time.

What would Grandma think of Mr. Britt? the thought occurs to me suddenly. Probably not much. Maybe she'd be sorry for him and tell him he needs to go to the beach more often, or at least build himself a sandbox.

Then I wonder: why would a woman like that marry a man anything at all like Mr. Britt? She wouldn't.

Now I know I can look at that poem of my grandpa's hanging on the wall.

spring

SOMEHOW IT JUST DOESN'T SEEM RIGHT. Grandpa's poem, that is. I'm trying hard not to think of the word Sunset, but I'm disappointed. I suppose it's not that bad really, but it's not what I expected to be born of a carpenter's pencil.

The poem is somewhere between what I was most afraid of and what I was hoping for.

Mum must have framed it as she found it, because it's in handwriting on a piece of raggedy paper torn around the edges—unless Mum did that to be artistic or something. It took me awhile to read the writing. It's scrawly and thick in places because of the pencil, and some of Grandpa's "e's" are so big that they loop up like "l's". And yeah, he mentions roses and spring. I wish he hadn't.

I read it again.

> It is the end of our summer
> —Spring passed so quickly
> And the petals of that rosebush
> We shared
> Are on the ground
> Dark and red and dark
> So red they are almost black
> In the rains.

And that's it. I wonder why he wrote "rains" instead of "rain." Maybe it was a mistake. And those dark red petals in the puddles of rain—I picture them as blood. I look at the date again. September 19, 1917. Wait a minute! Grandpa would have been...fifteen! What was he doing writing a romantic poem when he was my age? What fifteen-year-old boy shares a rosebush with a girl? I wonder what Mr. Britt would say to this?

Most of the last line is ripped, but there's enough left of the letters to know what the words are. On second thought Grandpa must have torn it; Mum wouldn't have done this.

Mum isn't home. The house is quiet. Then there's the sound of hum and thump, hum and thump. Someone is on the half-pipe.

I grab my kneepads and helmet as I go out the back door, expecting to see Roland. It's Couch.

He ignores me as he rides. He's not doing anything fancy, just turning and moving. Finally he stops on the platform.

"You gotta get another platform, Kidd. I almost lost it at the other end—I almost flew over."

"Guess I'll have to make another twenty bucks so I can afford another platform, eh Couch?"

He drops in off the summit and speeds to the other side, the roaring buzz of his tires too loud to keep talking.

He keeps going and going, faster and faster. I watch him, almost hypnotized. I swing my head from one side to the other and don't even notice Roland drag his bike up beside me, until he reaches out and touches my arm.

I turn and watch as he adjusts his tie.

"Looks like Couch has come back," he says softly, as he pulls his toque off, scratches his head, puts it back on.

I nod. "Yeah."

Couch stops suddenly, and pedals backwards toward us. "What're you two mumbling about? Or is it another secret? I never know what's going on around here." He stops just before his rear tire drops off the edge. But he doesn't wait for answers. He turns his back to us, pedals forward and away. "I'm going to do a fakie!" he announces, and we watch as he builds up speed and wheels straight up the end of the pipe, rides off the top and comes back down with a thump, pedalling backwards. He doesn't quite get his balance though, and wipes out. He pulls the bike out from under his leg, curses, and climbs on again. He's about to make another try, but stops and looks at us standing there. Looks at me.

He picks up his bike, pushes through the cedar hedge, and and is gone without saying goodbye.

Roland doesn't bother taking off his toque this time: he just scratches at his head through the wool.

"Couch'll come around," he says.

"Maybe."

Roland looks at me and tugs on his tie as if he'd like to take it off, but can't.

MUM'S READING IN HER BEDROOM when I turn the TV off to go to bed. I read Grandpa's poem once again before walking up the stairs.

"Mum?" I knock gently on her cracked-open door.

"Come in."

"Where did you find that poem of Grandpa's?" I ask.

"You read it? The poem about the rain?"

I nod. "The *rains*."

She seems surprised. "Rains?"

"Yeah, rains."

"Really? You noticed that." She reaches for her old terry cloth robe waiting on the back of a chair by her bed. It should be threadbare by now, but over the years the nubbly threads have grown rougher and put up a good fight not to be thrown in the rag box. That robe's been around long enough for me to remember burying my face in it after a few lousy days at elementary school.

"Grandpa's stuff is in the attic, in the old trunk."

I don't mean to be rude, but with my toe, I push the chair and the robe out of Mum's reach. "It's okay, Mum. I don't need to look at Grandpa's poems right now. It was just curiosity, that's all."

"Oh, I like curiosity!" says Mum. Of course.

"Really, Mum. Get back into bed. Finish your book. I'm going to bed myself." I do the pretend-yawn thing, which never fools Mum, but she must really want to read. She snuggles back under the red-and-white quilt, props the book up, and finds her page.

I lean over and kiss the top of her head. "Goodnight, Mum."

"Goodnight, Ogilvie. And thank you for the gift certificate." She holds up the book she must have bought from BONNIE'S BOOKS.

The title: *Discovering the Artist Within*.

I hope that's not for me.

THE ATTIC IS MUM'S PLACE. I haven't been there since I was a kid. I don't remember where anything is, though I do remember coming up here to listen to the rain on the roof or the silence of heavy snow on the shingles.

There are bolts of fabric everywhere, remnants of almost everything Mum's worked on in the past ten years, cans of paint, varnish, pots of paste wax, and great stacks of decorating and furniture magazines, piled waist high. When I was little I thought Santa's elves came to work in our attic: it seemed to be the kind of place they would like. Sometimes I'd wake up late at night in November and December, and I was sure I heard their voices and footsteps, but it was probably just mice in the walls.

I don't see the trunk. Perhaps it's under the eaves. I follow the corners of the attic in the light from the one bare bulb and there it is, in a far dark corner. The light doesn't reach this far. I open the heavy lid. It's darker inside.

I remember all the little shelves that Mum has nailed between the two-by-four studs and reach up to the wall behind the trunk. Sure enough: there's a shelf, and I feel a smooth rounded shape, a candle, and next to it a matchbox with scratchy sides.

I light the candle—a white utility one—with a wooden matchstick, and the sulphur fills my nose. I drip some wax onto the tea saucer that Mum has left on the shelf and push the candle onto it.

There's a blanket folded over the stuff inside the trunk, and I pull this out and wrap it around my shoulders. The heavy grey wool is rough around my neck.

Underneath the blanket are photo albums, not like now with plastic covers and sticky pages, but with black paper pages and silver and gold corners. I've seen these photos before. They're not what I'm looking for, so I pull them out and stack them to one side.

Then there's clothing: a christening gown, creased and yellow; Grandma's cream-coloured wedding outfit—a skirt and blouse; and wrapped in tissue paper, a maroon tie. I pick it up carefully. This must have been Grandpa's tie. I don't know how to knot it, but I hang it around my neck anyway.

There are three thick crackly-plastic bags of Christmas-past cards. Strange things to keep for so long. And there is a wooden box that I have to lift completely out of the trunk to open. The lid slides out sideways. It is filled with papers. This must be it. Grandpa's poem stash. The writing on the piece of paper on the very top matches the writing downstairs in the red frame.

I put everything back in the trunk except the box. This I'll take downstairs where it's warm.

Spring rain starts to fall on the shingles of the roof as I blow out the candle and go down the steep narrow stairs back to my room. Mum can't hear my feet in woolly socks.

In the attic, the box looked like it belonged, but here with posters of freestylers and skateboard freaks on the walls, it looks strange.

I open it again, and play that game I used to play when Mum read a big night-time storybook to me. I reach into the box, not looking, and pull out a piece of paper.

I see the pencil scrawls I expect to and it looks like a poem—short lines all the way down the left side of the page—but it's a list.

two pounds beef
two pounds pork
onions
milk
eggs

and a bunch of other stuff. Why wasn't this thrown out?

Close my eyes again and reach for another paper.

I open them and see the word skate. It's not a word I expect.

It's called "The Last Game."

The skate blades swing from my shoulder
Pendulums nudge my elbow
> *Time passes as ice melts in low spring sun.*
> *Hurry! for the last game.*

Laces snap after a long season
In my still-cold fingers
I tie them short at my ankles
> *Strong now.*

Push onto the ice
With its gentle sound of small waves
To one side then the other as I stroke
To the end
Guiding the frozen disc in front of me.

Slap
and Spray
To the net.

The horse-manure puck waits
Sinking in warm ice
And I try to think how glad I will be of the pond in
mid-July
But this is it—

The last game.

I close the box slowly. The wooden lid catches in splinters.

I reread "The Last Game."

Funny how suddenly light I feel. As if I'm floating on an outdoor ice rink in some small town outside Winnipeg. It's the early 1900s. I see Grandpa in baggy sweater and high socks, strands of wool unravelling. I see him young—fifteen even—with his head bare, ears red in the cold, pushing a frozen horse bun in place of a puck, down spring ice to a net, handmade and mended. I hear the shouts of other players—"Pass it here!"—and hear the cheers of girls with mittens and numb toes, watching boys who will not be heroes again until November.

I fold the paper as I found it and put it on the desk beside my bed. Not until I turn the light off and pull my quilt up around my ears—still cold from the attic—do I realize something that's quite obvious.

Grandpa wrote a hockey poem! No sunsets, no roses, not even a petal. Okay, so it was about Spring, but a different kind of Spring.

What would Mr. Britt think?

I WAKE UP SMILING, my face stretching, my ears feeling far apart. What's this all about?

Then I remember: the hockey poem and Mr. B. Ha!

I put the poem back in the box, close it, and push it far under my bed.

seat belt

COUCH IS BUZZING WHEN I GET TO SCHOOL.

"Tony Jones is coming! Here! To our school!" He waves a bright green piece of paper. It's a notice he's obviously ripped from a bulletin board. "Look! A freestyle demo. In three weeks. Maybe we can meet him!"

He hands me the paper. He's so excited, he's shaking. He seems to have forgotten his anger.

Mallory turns around. Funny how she notices me now.

"Who's Tony Jones?" she asks.

"The hottest freestyler around!" says Couch.

"Cyclist?" she says.

Couch answers. "He's a bike *freak!* The stuff he can do! You should see...." His voice drifts off.

I break in. "He's from L.A."

"Los Angeles," she repeats in full. It's as if she wants to join our conversation but doesn't know what to say.

"Yeah—L.A." Couch is staring at her and she turns red. One problem with having such fine hair is that when you turn red, it's an all-over thing. I mean, her entire head is red, and even when she turns around to face the front of the room, with her back to us, we know she's still very red.

Mal bends over a book. I recognize it as her emergency book: the one she doesn't read but always looks at when she wants to seem busy.

"So what makes you think Tony would want to meet us, Couch?"

Ms. Potter swings the door open, comes in to the room, and Couch slides off the top of his desk and onto the seat with a thump.

"Why wouldn't he want to meet us? We have the only half-pipe in this town!" he hisses across the aisle.

"Yeah—a half-finished half-pipe." I watch Ms. Potter cross the room and arrange the stuff on her desk, but from the corner of my eye I see Couch smooth the green paper notice over the notebook on his desk.

Couch has got a point. Except for that rotting thing the municipality guys mistake for a skate park, mine is the only half-pipe in town, half finished or not. And Tony Jones has a reputation for hanging with the locals after a show. He's always interested in the spots in town: the pipes, walls—stairs like the cement ones outside the courthouse—and other shapes and drop-offs to do tricks on.

Under his breath, Couch calls to me. "What's the matter? You don't want to meet him?"

Ms. Potter is writing on the board and her chalk is louder than usual, scratchy and almost breaking on the "i" dots and the "t" crosses. She can hear our voices, I'm sure, but I guess she's decided to ignore us.

"Are you afraid someone's going to tell him you're a poet?" Couch grins like one of his own tattoo plans—not a pleasant thing to see.

63

"Why would someone do that? Hand me the paper!" I stretch towards Couch.

He does. "Here."

THE RAD TONY JONES HIMSELF
ON HIS
CYCLE THE WORLD TOUR.
AS SEEN EVERYWHERE.
HE'LL BE HERE!
WHERE YOU CAN SEE HIM.
JUNE 5TH. 3:00 PM.
BRING YOUR WHEELS....

Yeah, right. The gym is small: there wouldn't be room to move.

Suddenly I imagine what it'd be like with Tony and me out on the half-pipe.

Three weeks from now. I have to finish the pipe. Somehow.

Tony Jones doesn't have to know anything about the poem. I'll see to that.

MUM IS NOT A SNOOP. I know. I've had all sorts of things in my room and she's never found them. As far as I know, she's never even looked.

But today's the day she decides to strip my bed and vacuum the dust under it, and she finds Grandpa's box. Spring cleaning, she explains. Fair enough. It is spring.

Of course she's *delighted* to find that I've been reading Grandpa's poetry. And she's been busy, I see. The box is on the kitchen table when I come home from school, and beside it is a stack of soft cover books, all with the names of universities and colleges on them.

"There's some wonderful stuff in here, isn't there?" She pats the wooden box.

"I read one—the hockey poem," I say.

"Just one?"

"Just one." I look at the spines of those books. There must be one from every school on the continent.

Mum opens up her cigarette package and tries to sound casual. "I picked up these calendars today. Actually, I talked the librarian into letting me bring them home overnight." Her hand moves to the stack. "And look!" She holds up a brightly-coloured magazine. "This was delivered just today—it's the complete summer leisure program." She flips quickly through the pages. One page is dog-eared like a Saint Bernard. She pulls up the big flap, and reads the course description aloud: "Two-week day camp for artists of the future. Morning workshops in painting with oils, mime, *creative writing*...." She looks up at me. "It sounds wonderful, doesn't it? I would have loved such a thing when I was young."

"Well?" I say.

"Well what?"

"Why didn't you?"

She shakes her head. "We couldn't afford it. We didn't even have art class at my school. And writing! Writing was something we had to do in full sentences, and answers had to be written so that they repeated the question. There were no new questions, no stories, no poems...."

There she goes, I think. Mum on a tangent.

I try to bring her back. "Mum? Mum! Speaking of money—" okay, maybe that isn't the best way to introduce my topic—"I'd like to borrow a bit from you. I'll pay it back as soon as I can," I add quickly. Money's such a tough subject around here.

"What for?"

"The half-pipe. I'd like to finish it in the next few weeks. Tony Jones is coming to town." Even Mum knows who Tony Jones is.

Mum frowns, not in a bad way, but thinking. I feel hope. Then: "I can't, Ogilvie. It's spring—investment time of year. I haven't any cash."

She means garage sale time has come and people are getting rid of their old furniture and junk, and she has to buy it up to keep herself busy throughout the rest of the year.

"So you'd pay for some arts camp, but you won't loan me something for my half-pipe?" Maybe it's time I tell her how dangerous it is with only one platform.

She puts Grandpa's papers back in the box and slides the lid closed.

"It's different, Ogilvie. This could be your future."

I WAKE UP LATE AT NIGHT AGAIN. There's a light shining into my bedroom. It's the street light. They must have repaired it earlier in the day. I've forgotten how bright it is. It's been burned out for so long that sometimes I fall asleep with my curtains open. But now it's shining brightly and wakes me up, and I climb out of bed to close the curtains.

Instead I stand by the window and open it. The air is cold.

The half-pipe is a moonscape, the mid-section a shallow resting place between two craters. I could be Neil Armstrong out there, floating, floating, planting my flag.

The cedars move with a gust of wind and the light and shadows follow the motion. Fluorescent ghosts.

It's more eerie than beautiful. And Mr. Britt's probably asleep at this very moment and has no idea there's a moonscape in my side yard. Even if he saw it, I bet he'd only see a bulky plywood structure with splinters and mismatched patches of paint, ugly in the raw street light. To Mr. Britt.

No, I imagine that Mr. Britt gazes at the moon from the inside of thick glass, sitting at a little round table with a lace cloth and a candle on it. Not a utility candle. Something fancy.

I close my window, but leave the curtains open.

Somewhere around here I have some paper. Under a stack of freestyle magazines on the desk, which is supposed to be for doing homework.

The papers are covered with plans for the half-pipe. Scribblings and calculations for the curve of plywood, and diagrams. There's even a few of Couch's tattoo plans. Funny, how they turn up. But the back of the paper is empty.

Dear Mr. Britt,

Well, that's further than I got last time.

About your letter.

No, that's not right.

In regards to your letter.

No.

Your letter stinks.

No.

Makes me angry.

No. Well, yes, but no.

Okay, so it's true.

I stop writing. Outside, the new bulb in the street light flickers. I stare at the pale glow around it.

Maybe it's true. But I don't want it to be.

I stop again. This is ridiculous. That's not what I mean to say, and this start-stop-start-stop stuff—I can't get anything rolling here. No speed at all. I'm not getting any air.

There is something that might help. I put the papers aside and climb out of bed, walk down the hallway, the stairs, into the kitchen, and reach behind Grandpa's picture. I catch his eye in the black-and-white and he almost winks at me. Horse manure hockey puck, eh? I think, as I feel my fingers close around the flat and cut-away edges of the carpenter's pencil.

The papers crunch as I crawl back under the quilt, pull several pieces towards my propped-up knees. I write:

> *So maybe poetry is about beauty and love and maybe I can't know anything about that because I'm fifteen.*

Pause. I turn the pencil lead to a different angle. And continue.

> *But you see, the poem wasn't about poetry. It was about riding a bike. Maybe that's something that you haven't done for a long time. Maybe you don't remember what it's like. One thing I'm sure of,*

*you've never ridden a bike on a half-pipe
or up a wall or flown through the air.
Except maybe in a 747 with your seat
belt on.*

Then I hold the pencil for a long time and read over the words before I continue.

*Anyway, Mr. Britt, you have no more
to fear from me, The Ruffian. For I will
not be writing anymore poems, or anything else for that matter. You see, I have
a half-pipe to build and new tricks to
learn, and I am busy at school, learning
about beauty and love.*

I put the pencil on the paper, flatten my knees out, turn off the lamp beside my bed, and watch the half-pipe moon out my window. I imagine Tony Jones doing a back flip, his bicycle turning through the air in slow motion. He doesn't even thump when he lands—he just floats away, another guy on the moon. And I sleep.

I PUT THE LETTER IN AN ENVELOPE Monday morning and drop it off in the clunky mailbox at *The Optimist* on my way to school.

Mallory smiles at me, and Couch raises his brows, as if he's waiting for Mallory or me to speak before he does.

Today, before he has time to get angry, I say: "Got any ideas about how I can afford to finish the half-pipe?"

He shakes his head, but quickly grins.

Mallory turns her head. She's been listening again. "You could get a job." Just like that, and she turns around again.

Couch stares at the back of her head.

A job? And make enough money in three weeks to buy enough plywood, and have enough time left over to build the thing?

Sure.

GET A JOB. WHAT WORK CAN I DO? I think of the stores in town. Maybe a sandwich place or the burger joint.

First I should figure out how much I need. If I spend the twenty dollars from *The Optimist* on two-by-fours for the addition...and I also have the two sheets of plywood from Roland...I'll need another fourteen sheets at least. Eight dollars each...that's one hundred and twelve dollars...It could also use a new paint job—some heavy-duty outdoor paint. The half-pipe should look good for Tony Jones.

I could work at the lumberyard.

No. I only know about plywood. And not much about that.

Maybe I can write poetry for the newspaper! Ha!

So much for Mallory. *You could get a job.* What does she know?

IT'S NOT EASY TO CARRY A LOAD of two-meter-long two-by-fours on the cranky old Tin-Speed. I pull them across the handlebars, over one knee sticking out to the side, pedal with one foot, and take back streets. No one wants to pass me.

But it's a satisfying sound, the two-by-fours tumbling onto the wooden platform of my half-pipe. Twenty dollars is gone, but I have the forms, the beginnings of my extension.

A FEW TIMES I'VE GONE TO COUCH'S HOUSE on Tuesday nights without him mentioning it beforehand, and he and his dad and the tuna casserole are there expecting me. But after last week, I think I'd better wait.

I sit in the hallway, back against my locker, legs stretched out on the floor. Mallory almost trips over my feet as she comes around the corner.

"Hi," she says, stops.

"Hi."

There's the noise of people coming down the hallway: some of Couch's old teammates, I recognize. And he's with them. For the first time that I've seen since he's been off the team.

"Yeah—we're going to Wesley's to see the game," someone says. "His mum just bought a big-screen."

And someone else: "The Oilers are gonna do it this year."

"Not a chance. The Islanders, man."

Couch sees me and stops, almost bumps into Mallory. The other guys keep moving, don't seem to notice he's not with them, until one—Rick, I think—turns and yells. "Hey, Couch! Is that your girl, man? It's about time!"

Mallory starts to say, "I'm not..." but Rick's

fallen into step with the others, who are laughing.

When I look at Couch, he's got a look like a crow about to pluck out eyeballs. And something else.

Couch is red. I mean, Red.

"Just ignore them." I stand.

Couch ignores me. Mallory is right in front of his locker.

"I'd like to get into my locker," he says finally, and Mallory scrambles out of his way.

He slams the metal door back, and it echoes down the length of hall.

He drops his books inside. "My dad's away for the week," he says. "I'm eating at a neighbour's." He snaps the lock, and starts to walk away with empty hands. "Besides, you seem to be busy."

WEDNESDAY.

The paper and the classifieds. Maybe someone looking for someone to do something.

Pool cleaning.

The sandwich/salad place. Daytime shift. Nope.

Odd Jobs.

That might be something.

I dial the number.

"Hello. MacPherson House."

MacPherson House? That's the old folks' home around the corner from the park.

"Hi—I'm calling about your ad—Odd Jobs."

"Oh yes—can you come right over tomorrow after school?"

I don't think my voice sounds that young, but maybe so.

72

"Sure."

"I'm Miss Gordon—ask for me."

"Who was that?" Mum comes into the kitchen, peers over her armful of upholstery fabric.

"Miss Gordon. I'm going to do odd jobs at MacPherson House."

"Oh." Mum lets the bolt of fabric fall to the table with a heavy thud, and she stands there glowering at it, as if trying to remember what she wanted to do with the material. "Odd jobs," she repeats. She sniffs.

Maybe this isn't her idea of an opportunity.

necktie

"HERE'S A LIST," MISS GORDON SAYS and hands me a piece of paper.

"Do these things as you have time, keep track of how long it takes you, and give me the number of hours at the end of the week. There's a shed in back—that's where the lawn mower is—and first priority is to clean the stuff from beside the shed. Put it in the back of the truck to take to the dump."

I decide not to tell her that I don't have my driver's license. Maybe she doesn't expect me to take the stuff to the dump. First things first.

Behind MacPherson House there's a large vegetable garden, a few horseshoe pits, and next to them, a yard of thick grass and trees. Between the pits and the yard, there's a shed with a mossy roof. And on the far side is a stack of stuff that looks as if it's been piling up for several years.

The last thing to be thrown on is this year's first grass cuttings. I find a bag in the shed and shovel the grass into it. Then there are some old chrome chairs that have lost their seats. I carry them to the truck, a black-and-rust pickup, parked on the road. Last fall's leaves are next, old canning jars, most of them cracked or chipped, and something under a ragged tarp. I pull the tarp off, and I know how Mum feels on Spring Clean-up Garbage Day, when she cycles around the neighbourhood and finds pieces of furniture that people are throwing away.

Under that tarp is a stack of plywood. Probably almost exactly the amount I need.

Then I start to breathe again and think, surely Miss Gordon couldn't have meant that this plywood is for the dump? So it is a little soggy, springy even, but perfect for me, for shaping the curving walls of my half-pipe.

I run towards the back door of MacPherson House, pound up the wheelchair ramp, spring open the screen door. "Miss Gordon?"

"Sshh!" she motions me to be quiet. "There are people trying to relax here." But she doesn't seem bothered.

"That plywood—beside the shed—is it going to the dump too?"

"Everything beside the shed, didn't I say?"

"Yes, you did...."

"Then it's going."

"Can I have it?"

"Take it home." She waves me out the door.

I stand in the doorway. "Miss Gordon?"

"Hm?"

"I...uh...won't have my license for another year."

"Oh."

I think fast. "My Mum can drive."

She nods. "All right."

Yes!

Plywood!

Everything on the list is done before I leave that day.

I phone Mum to see if she can pick me up and take the rest of the stuff to the dump. "I'll be over on my bike," she says quickly. Maybe she's getting used to the idea of me earning money for the half-pipe.

Miss Gordon tells me to wait in the rec room down the hall.

The rec room is a big sunny place filled with women and men, with the click of needles and the gentle chug-chug of a computer booting up. One man, knitting something black, grins at me. Two men in golf caps and wheelchairs prepare to play computer golf. I notice one woman with faded red hair, wearing a green bathrobe and a purple beret. There's a sprig of plastic holly pinned to it. I sit on a chair left by the door and watch her, bent over a table and fitting pine cones to a Christmas wreath form. I shake my head—it's almost summer.

"What are you making?" I ask the man who's knitting.

He holds it up. "A cardigan. I figure it'll take me till fall to finish it, and the horseshoe championships are in September. I want to wear it then. It's often a little nippy in September, you know, and between shoes you tend to stand around a lot and pick up the chill."

I nod as if I know exactly what he's talking about.

"You like black?" I ask.

He pats the knitted piece. "I wear black during the years when the Stanley Cup isn't safely at home in Montreal."

"You're a Habs fan."

"You might say that," he says.

"You going to come here again?" he asks.

I nod. "This is my first day—doing clean-up. Odd jobs, they call it."

"Good," he says, and holds out his hand. I shake it. "Maybe some time I can show you how to knit."

"Maybe."

Mum walks in, sweating from her bike ride, and clutching a piece of paper in one hand. She looks happy. "What an opportunity. A truck! Do you think Miss Gordon will mind if I pick up a chesterfield on..." She looks at the paper..."Whitworth Avenue?"

Miss Gordon is standing in the doorway. "No, I don't mind at all. Just get rid of all that junk and take the plywood home." She goes away down the hall.

Mum looks at me. "Plywood?"

"Enough for my half-pipe."

"Wow. A bonus on your first day of the job. Does Miss Gordon know why you wanted the job?"

"Not exactly."

"Are you going to come back?"

I look at the woman with the wreath and the old man in mourning for the Habs. I don't think I'll take him up on his offer to teach me to knit, but even so, this could be interesting. "Next week, Miss Gordon will have another list of stuff that needs to be done. I'll come back."

"Well, you can always help me out with the tuition for camp!" Mum's so chirpy. She quickly adds, "Just joking!"

I don't think so.

I SPEND THE NEXT WEEK WORKING on the forms of the half-pipe. I think about Tony Jones and his back flip. And I keep thinking, "Only two more weeks, only ten more days."

Mum keeps busy with the new-old chesterfield, and sorting through Grandpa's poems, trying to arrange them chronologically, she says. I think she's hoping I'll read more.

Mum's made another frame, this one for a drawing of Grandma's. I suggested she make one more frame and take a photo of the Mad Hatter chair I like so much, and hang that on the wall. The owner is going to pick it up soon, and like all of Mum's pieces, we'll never see it again. A lot of Mum's work is like sculpture—such colours and shapes. I think she's happy I suggested she put a picture of her work on the wall, even though she said no, it doesn't belong with the poetry and drawing.

There's another reason I don't want to read Grandpa's poems now: those words that travel in my mind and pop out, well, they haven't been around quite so much in the past week. Or maybe I'm too busy to notice them. I figure, if I stop thinking about them, and if I stop thinking about Ms. Potter and Mum and even Grandpa, then maybe the words'll go away altogether.

Tony Jones is coming. Tony Jones is coming.

T.C. NIGHT.
> Comes and goes.
> Not a word from Couch.

THIS IS IT. THE COUNTDOWN. One more week. It'll take two or three days just to paint—two coats, twenty-four hours in between. Monday I'll work at MacPherson House, and maybe do a bit of work on the half-pipe, Tuesday and Wednesday after school I'll put the plywood on the frame, and Thursday and Friday, I'll paint. I've got it all worked out.

MISS GORDON HAS A LONG LIST of stuff for me to do Monday after school. Forget having time for the half-pipe. Once again I have to phone Mum to drive the old pickup truck. Some glasses and plates have to be returned to a rental place in town. Mum's a bit late meeting me, but when she does, she takes one look at the rec room and says she'll return the stuff on her own without my help. "You'll be busy enough!"

Looks like a lot of people had a party in this place. Miss Gordon explains that it's their big spring "do," when everyone dresses fancy, and eats and dances. The room is a mess. There's even a broken window!

But in the middle of the mess are the same people who were here last time: the woman making Christmas wreaths with pine cones—though her holly-sprigged beret is askew—and the old man knitting his black cardigan. As soon as he sees me, he grins. And there are the same two guys with their golf caps on, sitting in their wheelchairs in front of the computer, studying the meters left between the golf green and their balls—the white dots on the screen.

One of them presses the button on the mouse and waves his arm in the air as the computer ball sounds a satisfying clunk in the hole.

Except for the grin from the knitter, no one pays any attention to me as I empty the trash can full of paper tablecloths, napkins, bits of more than one broken plate.

When Mum comes back, I still have three items on the list.

> vacuum entrance hallway.
> put records and cassette tapes away.
> tape up window.

Mum helps with the vacuuming, but it's after dinner time and dusk when we get home, and the half-pipe waits.

IN ENGLISH CLASS, COUCH'S DESK IS EMPTY. He's missing a lot of English again. Across the board, Ms. Potter has written: CHESTER FIELD—SEE MR. TREVITT. TODAY. 3:30.

And she paces in front of his desk for a few minutes at the beginning of class. Then she looks directly at me. Today I'm ready for her and I look away first. She sighs loudly.

I wonder if he'll show up for lunch.

ROLAND FOLLOWS ME as I head down the hall after class and, sure enough, Couch's rear end's sticking out of his locker, a pile of sneakers and stained T-shirts beside his feet.

"Oh, Chester! I'd like to speak with you for a moment," says Roland in a high voice with just a hint of New England accent. He sounds amazingly like Ms. Potter. I start to laugh.

Couch stands up straight quickly, smashes his head on the shelf in his locker, and turns to face us. "Hey!" His face is red with anger. I move closer, almost between them, but Roland pushes me away gently and seems to be waiting for Couch to let it fly, or speak.

"What's the big idea?" Couch speaks loudly.

"Nothing, really." Roland turns to his own locker, number 673, and twirls the combination. "Just reminding you about English class, that's all. Ms. Potter wants you to see Mr. Trevitt today."

"I don't need reminding. I don't visit the principal—not even to pick up cheques!" Couch's voice has lowered, and now it's more like a growl.

Roland isn't teasing anymore. "There's an exam in a couple of weeks, Couch. Maybe I can go over some stuff with you."

"Thank you for your concern, but I'm kinda busy these days." Couch crawls back inside his locker and continues his search for coins. "Nice to know you have nothing better to do than study for a boring exam, Roland!" His words echo in the metal.

Roland pauses and his face narrows. Couch's words seem to have hit some mark. Then Roland shakes his head and he leans over. "Maybe Og can help you study."

Now I feel like hitting Roland myself. Why'd he say that?

"You mean the Poet-King-Cupid-with-his-head-in-the-clouds?" More echoing words, but without the angry tone. Couch sounds like he's just really frustrated.

I grab Roland's elbow, pull him back, and shake my head. "Enough, already."

"Okay," Roland says. He seems relieved to give up, and nudges Couch's backside with his toe. "Let's get some lunch, Couch. Face it: there's nothing in there."

"There is." Couch straightens finally, and he flips a few loonies in his hand. They jingle into his pocket as they meet other coins. "I'm starving," he says, and leads the way to the cafeteria, a noisy, greasy place, that always makes me wish I could carry a lunchbox with the aplomb that Roland does. But instead, I smuggle in the sandwich and apple that Mum's put in a paper bag and buy some fries with vinegar.

There aren't many seats left today. It's always that way when Couch decides to excavate his locker and makes us late. I notice a few seats around Mallory. She looks up from her book, looks at me, at Couch, then quickly away.

"Here!" I pull a chair out from a nearby table, right in front of Roland's path. He almost falls over my outstretched arm.

"We need one more chair," he points out, and goes around to Mallory's table, pulls one out from there. She peers at him through her thin fringe of hair. Her bangs are so fine she can't possibly hide behind them like some girls do.

Again, she looks at me for a second, then away.

We sit down. I sit with my back to her. I'm not sure why I do. My pepper salami sandwich tastes stale even though it's not, and I leave my apple on the table. Couch sits across from me. He'll pick the apple up. Roland goes to get us fries. Once in awhile he has fries too. I think smelling mine every day gets to him.

"This is going to be the longest NHL season ever!" Couch talks with his mouth full of yogurt. "You know, the final game of the Stanley Cup used to be in March? Amazing, isn't it? Hey—have you made up your mind about hockey camp? You coming or what?"

I shake my head. "Can't afford it. Mum won't even loan me money for the half-pipe."

Couch's face stretches out long, then suddenly adjusts to its normal proportions. "Maybe we could work something out with Dad."

I shake my head again. Mum would never go for that. Couch knows it too.

"Yeah, yeah, I know." His face begins to stretch again. Man, nobody can do Disappointment like Couch can. "Talk to your Mum," he says. "You gotta come with me. All the guys from the team are gonna be there...."

Is he trying to tell me he doesn't want to be on his own with them?

"Couch, I'm a lousy hockey player."

"Nah—you're a natural. In a couple of years, maybe we can laugh at you, but you're not so bad now. Come with me."

"I'll think about it."

He sits back. "Yeah—I forgot. You're into *other* things now."

I try to ignore the sarcasm, the sudden anger, in his voice. "There *are* other things, you know," I say.

He stares at me.

The pepper in my salami must be hotter than usual. "There are things besides sports. "I take another bite before I cool down.

"Yeah—well," is all Couch says. "Keep thinking about the camp. Maybe you *need* to come."

"Hi." I hear a voice behind me, and it's a relief to turn away. It's Mallory. Couch spoons in more yogurt and says nothing.

She sits down, uninvited. Maybe she's not as shy as I always think. But maybe she is. She's red all over again.

She seems nervous and unsure what to do with her long arms; her narrow hands flutter over her crossed knee, the book bag at her side, the table. One hand hovers over the apple, hesitates, then returns to her knee.

"Go ahead," I say.

"May I?" She picks it up and her teeth crackle through the skin.

I know Couch wanted that apple. He should have grabbed it sooner. I also know how badly he wants me to go to that camp. Maybe I went too far about *other things....*

Mallory finishes chewing and swallows. "Ms. Potter told me there's going to be an after-school writing group next year. I thought you might like to know about it."

Couch leans forwards suddenly. "What's with poetry anyway? I mean, I've been reading those ads—you know, in the paper, people looking for people—and they all want someone who reads poetry ALOUD! I don't know anyone like that. Do you?" He stops, all at once, and scrapes his chair back away from the table. "Where's

Roland with those fries, anyway?" he says.

"I don't really write poetry," I say to Mallory, but loud enough for Couch to hear, even as he's walking away.

"And I'm not a poet."

Mallory has a funny look on her face—kind of crumpled up. Then she stands—jumps up—crashes her knee on the table leg.

"You okay?" I ask, but she's already halfway across the room. She almost smashes into Roland, but he steps aside, and she just catches his elbow as she goes by.

"Whew! What was all that about?" Roland asks, as he hands me the fries.

"Mallory was telling me about some writing group next year," I mumble.

"So? What'd you tell her? No? Is that why she was running away? Almost ran me down."

I shrug. "She got up pretty quickly."

Roland leans close, looks at me the way my doctor does when he stares down my throat. "I think Mallory likes you," he says.

"You're starting to sound like Couch," I say.

"Am I?" Roland raises his brows. "Think of that: Mr. Field and me with something in common—good. Maybe he has a point, Og."

"Yeah, well. He also seems to think I feel the same way about her."

"Maybe he has a point," Roland repeats. He bites off the head of a fry. "Maybe that's what's really bugging him. Hey...." He looks around. "Where'd Couch go anyway?"

"He went looking for you." I eat a couple of fries. They're cold.

Roland eats one more fry and pushes the rest

away, picks up a napkin, wipes each finger, and then carefully shreds the napkin. He clears his throat.

Okay. I'm waiting.

Clears it again.

"Roland, do you want to say something?" I ask. I hope it's nothing more about Mallory.

He pretends to be surprised at my question. "Well, I know you usually spend Tuesday nights with Couch and his dad, but I was wondering if you'd...come to my house." A long pause.

I don't answer because I'm thinking. There's no chance of T.C. Not after the last couple of weeks. But if Couch asks, it'll be important that I go. Maybe.

"It's my birthday," Roland interrupts, "and my mum's having a few...friends over."

The way he says friends I know that these guests are not Roland's friends. They must be his parents' friends.

"One of them..." now he sounds like he's choking, "one of them has a daughter. I think my mother's trying to set me up." His voice gives out completely and he stares at me with miserable eyes.

I hear Couch's size elevens hitting the floor behind me, coming close.

I should go to Roland's. I had no idea it was his birthday. I open my mouth to speak, just as Couch grabs his chair, turns it backwards, and straddles it, his arms crossed over the back.

"You're coming tonight, aren't you? Dad's really missed you the last two weeks." His eyes look dark, and his brows are up, as if he's asking for something more than a yes or no.

I wonder if he heard a word of what Roland was saying to me.

"Dad's making T.C.," Couch adds.

I look from one to the other and back again.

I stall. "I have to work on the half-pipe," I say. They both wait.

"I'll come when I'm finished." I look at Couch. Roland walks away, gripping the pointed end of his necktie.

scissors

OKAY. I'M IN MY OLD HIGH-TOPS. I have my hammer in hand. The phone rings.

I can hear the ring outside. I keep hammering. Mum comes to the door.

"Ogilvie. Phone for you. Sounds like a girl." She stretches her face into a question mark, but I ignore that.

"Yeah," I say, picking up the receiver.

"Ogilvie?" The voice is high and sounds like someone gasping for air. "Ogilvie? It's Mrs. Gilbert. You're a friend of my son's? Roland's?"

"Is he all right?"

There's the sound of a sniffle, then Mrs. Gilbert blows her nose. "Yes—he's all right. I think." She hesitates. "But maybe not....Can you come and speak to him?"

"What's happened?"

"He seems to be...sewing," is her answer. "And he has my big scissors! I'm so afraid of what he might do...." She hangs up suddenly.

ROLAND'S HOUSE ON THE CLIFF is a big box of a place. I've only been in it once. His mum doesn't trust people under the age of thirty, and she especially doesn't like them in her home. Except for Roland, I guess.

She doesn't even say hello to me as I walk through the doorway, and there's a funny expression on her face. A mixture of fear and anger and even...embarrassment.

"You're the only one I could think of—Roland talks about you all the time. I didn't want to call the police."

"The police?" The words are out of my mouth before I can think. It's hard to imagine a mother who would call the police. How serious is this?

"He has my big scissors. They're very sharp...like a knife...."

What is she saying?

"He might injure himself," she whispers.

Roland? Is she talking about the Roland I know?

"Roland's father is at a board meeting—in Toronto. You're the only person I could think of to call." She leads me down the hallway to the double doors opening into the dining room. At arm's length and with a soft movement of her wrist, she pushes open the door.

Roland has taken over the formal dining room with its dark red velvet walls. The room is covered in fabrics, but these fabrics are curtains and bedspreads and, on top of the pile, a brocade tablecloth. Or rather, what's left of a brocade tablecloth. Every piece of fabric has long sections cut out.

"Diagonally," Roland cries out when he sees me. "Ties must be cut on the bias." He waves the biggest shears I've ever seen—yeah, they look sharp—and as he does, I hear a quick intake of breath from his mum. Or maybe it's the sound of choking. Roland doesn't seem to notice.

"Ties must be cut on the bias—that's why I need all this fabric. I can't go to the store and ask for one-tenth of a meter of fabric. I need at least one and a half meters. I need the curtains, I need the velvet spread. And that's why I need this!" He holds up the tablecloth and peers through a tie-shaped opening in the fabric.

Mrs. Gilbert bursts into tears and puts a hand on my arm, a wide hand with long fingers and square knuckles. A strong hand, yet at the end of each finger there's a flimsy oil-slick-pink nail, filed to a point. Her fingers tighten as she says, "You talk to him." Her other hand pushes me. I can feel four filed points at my back. Then she leaves.

Roland dashes across the room and closes the door behind her with a flourish. He turns to me.

"What do you think, Mr. Kidd?" he asks. There's a floor lamp next to the sewing machine and instead of turning on the overhead lights, he pulls the shade off the lamp and moves the stand like a singer holding a microphone might, casting a bright spotlight over the velvet walls.

Now I see that the walls are covered in ties, tacked on with bulletin-board pins. Two of them I recognize as the fabric of Roland's old private school blazers. One looks like it might be from one of his father's suits. And one is made from a very heavy flowered satin with thick gold threads shot through it. I hate to think what that comes from.

"Roland. What's happening?" I wish he'd put

the shears down before his mum left the room. Might have calmed her a little.

"This is it, Mr. Kidd. I've found my calling. I'm going to design ties."

I try again. "No. I mean, what's happening...to you?"

"I tell you, Mr. Kidd. This is my vocation."

Am I making sense?

Maybe I am. For a brief moment he is still. "Oh, I see what you're asking. Where did this part of me come from? I don't know. I think it has something to do with last September, when I realized I couldn't live without a tie. A tie is part of my life. That's how it is."

"What about everything else?"

"What else?"

"All those A's at school...."

One corner of his mouth turns up. "Yeah. Those. What about them?"

"Well, what happens to them? Now that you're going to design ties?"

"Nothing happens to them. I'll always learn and read. Always have. That's just who I am. And I'm also going to design ties. Here!" He reaches for a piece of purple. "This could be for you. It could be a poet tie!"

"I'm not a poet," I say.

"Fine. I'll make it for when you realize you are!" He moves close to me and throws the fabric over my head. I step back but not before he manages to loop it around my neck like a scarf. "There! You see," he says, and runs back to the far end of the table.

"Now this!" And he picks up a piece of terry

cloth. I notice the old bath towel it's been cut from, lying on the table.

"Look at this. A fine early morning tie—something a fellow can wear in the shower if he really feels naked without a tie, and if, for him, feeling naked is not such a great feeling."

I have the feeling that some part of him is standing back, laughing at me, at his mum. And I kind of like this loud and dramatic Roland. The part of him that was miserable and asking me to his birthday doesn't seem to be around at all, but the quiet Roland is still here—maybe that's who's laughing—and the helpful Roland is too. I'm not sure if Mr. and Mrs. Gilbert are going to understand this part of Roland any better than they understand any other part. One thing I know, though: "You're not going to kill yourself, are you?"

He looks amazed. "Kill myself? Whatever gave you that idea, Mr. Kidd?"

"That's what your mum thinks."

"She does?" His eyes almost cross as he looks down to knot the terry cloth, and his voice lowers. "This tie thing's been bugging me for a long time now, Mr. Kidd. Sometimes I've wondered what it'd be like to...you know...but I've only wondered because...I've wondered if anyone would notice if I just wasn't here anymore. I've even wondered if I'd notice if I wasn't here anymore. That's what makes this tie thing so important." His voice picks up. "Maybe to you, it's just me designing ties. And to my mum, it's me going crazy, but to me it's how I know I'm here."

My friend is shaking. I put my hand out to him.

"Roland—you've got to calm down. A bit, anyway."

He looks at me squarely then. "You think a bit will be enough? Enough for my mum?"

"I hope so," I say. "She's really freaked."

"Hmm." He picks up the shears, holds them at eye level, looks at them.

I think I can hear someone breathe carefully on the other side of the door.

He puts the shears on the table. "Maybe I can clean this up—move it to my room."

"That would be a start."

"Maybe I should buy Mum a new tablecloth."

"That would be an idea."

His voice softens. "Something with purple— an eggplant pattern maybe—and olives, to go with my toque."

"Roland!"

He starts to put the lid on the sewing machine, then folds up the remnants of fabric.

His voice is very steady. Normal. "Maybe I can wear this to school." He pats the bath-towel tie around his neck. Another sound at the door—a sort of hiccough.

"Mum! You can come in now!" Roland calls.

The door opens and Mrs. Gilbert stands in the doorway, staring at the terry cloth around Roland's neck.

"I have some birthday guests to cancel." She speaks loudly. I get the feeling she wants me to go now.

"Oh, yeah. Your birthday," I say to Roland. And a thought passes through my mind: would this have happened if I'd turned down Couch, and said yes to Roland?

Roland grins and reaches up to pat my shoulder, as if he's the tall one, and he says, "I'm glad you came to my party, Mr. Kidd. Best one I've ever had. Next time maybe we can cut some cake."

His mum sort of shudders then, and she moves to the front door and holds it open. "Thank you," she says to me, and she's stiff as a blue popsicle.

I look at Roland, standing behind her. His grin is half gone, but I think he'll be okay. Something about his eyes now. He looks like he's freed himself in some way.

RING.

Ring.

Ring.

No one's answering the phone at Couch's house. Maybe I pushed the wrong number.

I try again. This time Couch picks up on the first ring.

"Yeah," he says.

"Sorry I missed T.C."

"Yeah—that's too bad." He sounds like he's about to hang up.

"Couch," I say quickly. "An emergency came up."

"An emergency," he says. "I know about your emergency. Gotta go now. Bye."

Maybe he and his dad were just at the best part of the movie. Maybe he didn't want to miss it, so he had to hang up quickly. Maybe.

ROLAND'S NOT AT SCHOOL. After school, I phone Mum, then grab the Tin-Speed and race over to Roland's house.

Roland himself answers the door, but his mother has well-developed helicopter-ability, and hovers over him.

"Mr. Kidd!" he greets me, and for a split second I see him as he was yesterday. Then his voice lowers. "Og!" he says now.

"Hey, Roland."

Mrs. Gilbert looks at me: at my cap, my *Wheel Thing* T-shirt, my shoes, which are muddy, though I haven't noticed until now.

"I think I'll go pick up groceries for dinner, Roland." She gives me a funny look, as if we have a secret or something, and I feel like I've just been interviewed for a baby-sitting job. Guess I look more trustworthy than I suddenly feel.

She leaves, fussing with her keys, and Roland leads the way into the kitchen at the back of the house. I peek in the dining room as we pass. It's clean. Not a scrap of brocade or satin, not a pin on the wall. And the house is so still, like it's dead.

"How was school?" Roland is pouring himself a coffee. I help myself to a cola in the fridge.

"As always."

"Anything I should know about?"

"Stuff you probably know already."

He sits on the window seat. I sit on the other end. I can see a ferry docking.

I notice he's wearing the tie made of flowered satin with gold threads.

"Mother took me to a doctor today." He takes a careful sip. "He says I'm fine. Adolescent stress, that's what he said it was. Mother told him she'd read about that." Roland pulls his toque off, unrolls the cuff, and rolls it back up again.

I feel as if he's asking me something. But I'm not sure what. Maybe he's daring me to say that the doctor is wrong. Or that he's right.

Instead I say, "Good tie."

He fingers it. "It is, isn't it? Quite radical."

Actually, it doesn't seem radical at all—it seems quite normal suddenly.

And Thursday, Roland is back at school, at his locker, at all his usual places, and everything seems normal. Almost. I know I'm never going to see another of those plain navy ties again.

yellow grass

FRIDAY MORNING, Mum's wearing her determined face. She hands me an envelope. "This," she says, "is a cheque. Today is the last day of registration for the art camp. Before you know it, it'll be August."

(I'm glad she doesn't wag her finger at me.)

She's still holding it out. I stare at the white envelope. How much is the cheque written for?

"Well?" she says. She stuffs it into my pocket. "Take it. For me."

She turns around and bends over the hassock she's working on. She braces herself on it with one knee and pulls the old fabric away from the frame. The brocade is faded but tough, and the muscles bunch in her skinny arms. She sits back, choking, waving her hands through the ancient dust that flies up.

THE REC. CENTRE IS AROUND THE CORNER from school. The woman at the desk smiles at me. She has the tiniest Happy Face I've ever seen caught in a hole in her nose.

"Can I help you?"

"Yeah." I point to a poster on the wall. "The arts camp. I'm supposed to sign up for it."

"Supposed to?" She rubs her nose, and the Happy Face turns on its side. "People take English and Algebra at summer school because they're *supposed* to."

She's probably another person who would have loved this opportunity when she was young—and all that stuff.

I reach into my pocket, where the envelope is still crumpled, and pull it out, open it. One hundred and twenty dollars. Mum's going to spend one hundred and twenty dollars on something I don't want. I put the cheque on the counter, push it across the desk.

SCULPTURE. The word leaps out at me from a page of description laid out under the glass surface of the desk.

An introductory course. Work in the materials of your choice....

My eyes move to the price: fifty dollars, plus seventy dollars for supplies.

I jab at it with my finger. "This one. Register me in this one. The name is Felicia Kidd."

"Felicia?" Another nose rub, and Happy Face is on the top of his head.

She writes out the receipt and hands it to me, together with a pamphlet on the course. I crumple the paper into the same pocket that the cheque was in.

There you go, Mum.

For you.

AT HOME, MUM IS IN THE GARAGE spray-painting. I see the old blanket across the window as I walk up to the door.

"Just a sec!" she calls when I knock. Then, "Yeah?" And she pokes her head out the door, a mask over the bottom of her face.

My hand closes around the crumpled paper. "I signed up for a course."

She looks pleased. "You're going to enjoy that camp."

How can I tell her?

"I still think you'd enjoy it more than me." I pull the paper out. "I'll just leave the receipt on the bench here."

She nods, back at work.

She can find it later. Alone. I close the door behind me.

OKAY, THIS IS IT. This is really it.

I'm in the kitchen, swallowing milk. Mum hasn't come out of the garage yet, and she's been in there long enough to read the papers. But I've got work to do.

If I can get the plywood on tonight, maybe I'll be able to paint one coat before Tony Jones is here.

The screen door slams shut behind me and I round the corner to the half-pipe, the stack of plywood.

The plywood is gone.

I SEE THE THIEF AS AN OVER-SIZED CROW, carrying his treasure away. Hovering over it in his nest. Cawing at me, screeching with laughter.

How dare you?

In a few short long-June-days
yellow grass will
shake awake green
uncurl
forget even.

"Pretty quiet out here!" Mum is standing behind me on the other side of the platform. "I was expecting noise."

"So was I," I say, glad she's banished the words from my head again, relieved at the sudden emptiness.

Mum pads across the plywood in her old tennis shoes.

"Oh," she says quietly, when she reaches my side and sees the square of yellowed grass. "Oh."

"Oh," I echo.

"Who would do that?"

I shrug.

She sits down next to me. "That plywood was heavy."

"Mmm."

"Maybe it's not far. We could go and look for it."

Wow. Mum volunteering to help with the half-pipe. I should leap up. But I don't move. I can't.

Then she says: "I do know how hard you've worked for this, Ogilvie."

Mum's silent, thinking. "We could phone Mr. Field. He helped you the first time. He has a truck."

I shake my head. "I think I'd better give up this idea, Mum. It's too late."

Mum stares at me. "It's not too late. And *you* know that better than anyone." She smiles. That's probably as much as she's ever going to say about arts camp. I can only hope it's the end of Burr Lake too.

She follows me into the house and puts the kettle on for tea, arranges the tea things.

"Maybe you can help me with this then," she says at last, and sits at the table. Grandpa's poems are all over the piles of scraps, pincushions, news-papers, books, and usual stuff.

She puffs on her cigarette, puts it in the ash-tray, picks up a piece of paper, sets it on top of another. "It's really tough, putting these in some order."

The kettle whistles. I rinse the teapot in boil-ing water, put the bags in, fill it, put the cosy on. Can't believe I'm doing this. TONY JONES is com-ing to town, and I'm making TEA!

Behind me, the papers stop rustling. There's silence. "Here's something," says Mum. Silence again as she reads.

I fill two mugs. A little honey in Mum's.

I don't want to spend the night mucking around with Grandpa's poetry. Words that rattled in his head, like they do in mine. Except he put his on paper, like other poets. Now people have to read them. If he hadn't put them on paper, maybe the words would've stopped. Maybe they would've died and there would have been just silence in his head. Maybe he put them on paper, hoping that if he emptied his head, the words would leave. There's a certain number of them, and when you run out, they're gone. Or did he write them, hoping they'd go, and instead more words came and filled the empty spaces as soon as they went? And he wrote faster and faster, hoping they'd go, go, go, but they didn't.

"Really, Mum. I'm not interested." I set her mug down beside her elbow and carry mine to the window, where I stand, looking at the half-pipe.

Mum doesn't seem at all upset. She just continues as if she didn't hear.

"This is something. I think it's the second half of that poem in the hallway."

She sits taller in her chair.

"Ogilvie—fetch that poem please."

And I do.

Mum reads:

> *It is the end of our summer*
> *—Spring passed so quickly*
> *And the petals of that rosebush*
> *We shared*
> *Are on the ground*
> *Dark and red and dark*
> *So red they are almost black*
> *In the rains.*
> *They are maroon*
> *Like the necktie you wore*
> *That night*
> *You grew up...and away*
> *And I imagine your clothing, like the petals*
> *In a crumpled heap, somewhere on the other side*
> *Of another world*
> *—We used to giggle under the same quilt*
> *That necktie, and you, paraded so proudly*

You dangled me
Only twelve
Swinging from the silver tie-clip
I was angry with you, growing up.
Still am.
If you hadn't
We could still be us
Fifteen in dungarees,
Not you,
Eighteen,
Dead.

The maroon tie—the one I'd found in Grandpa's trunk, now hanging over the head of my bed—had belonged to his brother, the one who'd been killed in the war.

Mum speaks softly. "I guess that's what he meant by 'rains.' The rains of the Great War. It rained so much that Europe became a bath of mud and blood."

Suddenly, Mum stands up and starts picking up the papers, one after the other. All her careful order is now confusion. She crumples some as she pushes them into the box, slides the lid over, a few sticking out.

"Your grandpa never said much about my uncle John. He must have cared for him very much though." She blinks several times as she puts the box away on the shelf next to Grandpa's picture. The way she aligns it perfectly with the wall, I know she plans on leaving it there for awhile.

She turns around and pulls her sleeve across her face.

"Sometimes," she says hoarsely, "sometimes I

know why poetry scares you. Sometimes it scares me too."

She grabs her jacket. "Come for a walk with me, Ogilvie."

I grab my flannel shirt and pull it over my T-shirt. "Let's go find my plywood."

She nods.

We reach the gate in the cedar hedge and she says, "I forgot my cigarettes. Can you go back and fetch them, Ogilvie?"

I return to the warmth of the kitchen, and I feel like part of an audience, on stage after a performance, after everyone has left. I pick up Mum's cigarettes and her matches and stand in front of the stove, looking up at Grandpa's photo.

I remember how I felt when I first read that poem. Disappointment. A love poem. A spring love poem. Hello Mr. Britt, I'd thought, even though I fought not to.

Well, it was a love poem. But I'm not disappointed anymore.

I touch Grandpa, under the glass.

"IT CAN'T BE FAR," SAYS MUM, "unless of course the person had a vehicle."

I stop her and point to tracks on the outer side of the hedge, leading to the sidewalk. Two clear tire tracks, about half a meter apart. Mum bends over. "They might be dolly tracks. They must have slid the sheets between the trees and onto a dolly."

We keep walking, though I don't know why. The wood is probably far away. Obviously, the person was prepared.

Down around the corner, to the winding road that runs alongside the Fraser River—Mum's favourite road—towards Harbour Park.

Mum slows her usual speed. "You're right, you know. This is probably a waste of time."

But now I don't want to stop. We've come this far, and besides, the walk is helping to calm Mum's feelings about the poem, and the park is one of her favourite places. We continue in that direction.

And there they are. At first, for just a second, I think they're overturned picnic tables, but the tables are in their usual places. The sheets of plywood are leaning, individually, against the cottonwoods near the entrance to the park, and they look very bright and shiny. It's as if the person who took the wood wanted me to find them. I remember the words in my mind, about the giant crow stealing treasure.

We walk closer, and then I break into a run, to the nearest sheet.

Spray-paint. Bold, black-outlined, green and red. Stained-glass graffiti shouts at me.

POET FREAK   RHYMING DUDE
SUNSET MAN   COUPLET KIDD

Mum discovers why they're leaning as they are against the trees.

"The backs are painted too," she says. "They're almost dry." She holds up a finger with a faint red smudge.

I stare at that smudge for a long minute.

The tree over our heads rustles, and a crow flies away with a loud caw. I wish I could laugh or shout.

Instead, I reach to the ground for a rock and throw it after the bird, long gone.

Mum looks at me, surprised. "We've found your wood," she says.

"We have," I say.

Mum drags one piece towards the gate.

"Don't bother." I begin to walk out of the park, towards home.

She doesn't listen, sets the wood against the open gate, and stands back. "You know," she says, "I kind of like it. Reminds me of New York City. You're going to have a very urban half-pipe."

I turn back. "But read it, Mum."

Mum opens her mouth to say something, closes it, opens it again. "Tony Jones rides too fast to read," she says finally.

pirouette

I HOPE EVERYONE IN THE NEIGHBOURHOOD doesn't mind pounding nails at six in the morning. Bang bang. Bang. I'm ready for the plywood. It's thin, and has never dried out completely, so it curves easily into shape on the forms.

Mum reminds me that she has better things to do, but she does stand on the pieces for me, coffee cup in hand, as I tack them down with ring nails. She leaves when I begin to put screws through the wood.

I try to ignore the graffiti. It's so bright. All those words staring up at me. Bang! Like the words in my head. Bang bang! Bang.

Mum comes back with breakfast—a bagel with peanut butter and cream cheese. She doesn't ask how it's going. I can see her looking around, nodding, before she goes back in the house.

It's after lunch time when I'm finally putting the last screw into the top of one of the new platform extensions.

I wish I had the time to ride a bit myself. I run back and forth a couple of times just to feel the solidness of it. I can hardly wait to ride. For a second I think that even if Tony Jones doesn't come, this'll be enough: just to have my half-pipe finished.

No. Jones has to come!

"Yahooooo!" I holler as I slam through the screen door. Mum stands there as if she's been waiting for me.

"Here—have a sandwich before you go." She hands it to me, and then half turns away. "Maybe you should have a shower too!"

I grab the sandwich. "Mum! It's three o'clock. Tony Jones is probably walking through the gym door right now!"

She holds the door open. "Try not to stand too close to anyone." She laughs as the door closes.

I leap onto my bike—my real bike, not the Tin-Speed—and pedal to school.

There are bikes everywhere when I get there. Kids from every elementary school in town as well as the high school. I can't see Couch. He was probably the first person here and is right up at the front of the crowd. The gym is full. The five double doors are open, people pressing in. Little kids slip through legs. I'll never get to see Tony Jones. I manage to stick my head around the corner of a door, only because of my height. There are enough kids for a hockey team, watching from under my arched and twisted body. I feel like a bird-mother.

I hear a voice.

"Psst! Ogilvie! Up here!"

It's Mallory. She's lying on a tiny platform suspended above the curtains of the stage at one end of the gym. Her head looks out over the edge and she motions to me. She has the perfect view of the gym floor and Tony Jones.

It feels like I'm picking up that entire hockey team, and together, we're like a train with a snowplow. The crowd moves, not much but just enough for us. I let the kids off just in front of the stage, where they buzz and pop gum. Mallory points out the ladder behind the curtains and I climb up towards her.

"How'd you know about this?" I ask.

"I volunteer for the Shakespeare festival every spring. I was prompter last year. I lived up here for two weeks!"

I lie down on my stomach beside her and look down, but not before I realize I'm close enough to touch that soft hair of hers. I wish I'd taken Mum's suggestion to shower.

Again I look for Couch.

The crowd is starting to get noisy. Some are starting to chant, "JONES, TO-NY, JONES, TO-NY."

Mallory wiggles to be more comfortable.

"How long have you been here?"

"About an hour." She doesn't move her eyes from the floor.

"I wonder where Couch is."

"I thought he was the biggest fan."

"He is."

Mallory points suddenly and asks, "Is that Tony Jones?"

I look where she's pointing at a skinny guy in baggy shorts and T-shirt, with red kneepads. "That's him!" I say, and shiver. Where's Couch, anyway? He should be here.

Tony Jones circles around, pushing at the boundaries the crowd has left for him. They press back. Two guys, wearing JONES—CYCLE THE WORLD TOUR T-shirts, step into the clear space and pull a tarp off a mobile half-pipe at one end of the gym.

There's a groan from the crowd. Tony Jones stops circling, and stands with his bike between his legs.

The half-pipe must've been damaged when it was brought in. There are two enormous holes in the plywood. I watch Tony as he turns around. I can see his face as his lips curl and he blows angry breaths.

Suddenly he turns back, leaps onto his bike, and heads straight for the low ramp that's also been brought in and placed beside the half-pipe. Bang! He hits the ramp with ferocious speed, up onto the clean brick. He carves the wall and pulls off, drops back to the floor. Again and again. Ah! beautiful tread marks, I think, and catch sight of Mr. Trevitt's face near the doorway leading to the hall and the school office. A face in pain, mouth twisted. I grin and turn to Mal. She's staring at the principal too.

Then the show really begins.

"Wow! That's like an arabesque!" whispers Mal to me.

Tony Jones is standing on a rear peg, his other foot back, and pulling a wheelie.

"It's a peg wheelie," I say.

Tony Jones does a series of tailwhips, flipping the bike so neatly underneath his legs, then lifts a hand, waves at a few people in the front. He pulls the bike up onto the rear wheel and does a locomotive, standing with his foot on the peg, rolling, rolling backwards. Then he breaks into a quick spin. His red kneepads flash by. The crowd hollers, whistles, stamps.

I nudge Mallory and whisper, "Like a pirouette, isn't it!"

She nods, grins. Suddenly she points. "There's Couch."

I look. There he is, pressed against the wall. His head's moving like he's looking for something or someone. I wave my arm, but he doesn't see. I wave again. Yes—he sees. But he doesn't respond.

I look at Mallory. She looks at me. I know she's seen him too. We both wave to Couch. Now he turns away.

Mallory's biting her lip.

I give her a nudge, shrug. "I'll talk with him later."

The show ends sooner than I expect, probably because of the broken half-pipe. Jones is suddenly gone, and the crowd is wild, shouting for him.

I haven't really thought of how to tell him about my half-pipe. Somehow I'd imagined being able to simply meet him after the show, talk to him, say, "Hey man, come over," but I hadn't envisioned being in the rafters of the gym, and hundreds of people between us.

I join the crowd, shouting, "JONES, TO-NY, JONES, TO-NY." He's got to come back, ride more, let me have a chance to tell him. Maybe if I can signal to Couch. After all, he's down there. I can see the top of his cap, his ponytail pulled through the back.

It's so noisy.

The noise doesn't lessen as Jones returns, exhausted but waving. The shouting becomes a steady roar, and the crowd presses forward.

If I could get a note to him. I reach for my pockets and my elbow jostles Mal.

She looks at me, eyebrows raised.

My pockets are empty, except for the carpenter's pencil I used on the two-by-fours.

"Do you have paper?" I shout into her ear.

She nods, pulls her English notebook from where its been lying under her chest and rips out a page, but not before something flutters out onto the platform. A copy of my poem. She snatches it up and looks away.

I write:

> MY NAME IS OGILVIE KIDD. I
> LIVE AT 582 COLLINGWOOD
> CRESCENT. I HAVE A HALF-
> PIPE....

I rip the piece of paper in half, crumple the note. Start again on the other half.

> HALF-PIPE
> 582 Collingwood Crescent
> the KIDD

For a second I think of crumpling that too, throwing it like a ball, but it would be lost in the crowd, a piece of garbage. No doubt the floor will be littered with stuff when everyone leaves.

The music—though I can barely hear it—is almost at an end. He'll be leaving after that. He's tired. His feet are touching the floor more often now, his bike isn't quite as smooth as it was at first.

I fold the paper, make an airplane, and hold it above my shoulder and then let it go. The plane arcs across the gym, over Jones, past him. My stomach curls. The plane will disappear in the crowd. Jones is completing some trick I've missed entirely. Now he climbs onto the seat, bike in motion, puts one foot on the handlebars, then the other, finds his balance and stands. Just as the plane swoops down quickly, levels, floats...he reaches out and catches it, as if it was planned. The crowd goes crazy. Jones uses his free hand to reach down to the handlebar and flip himself off the bike. He stands, bike in one hand, my folded plane in the other. He bows low. For a second I think he's going to fly the plane back into the crowd—I hadn't thought of that—but no, he crumples it and shoves it in his pocket. Look at it! I want to scream.

I do. "Read it!" Over the din. And maybe he hears. He does look up.

I grin. Mallory waves. Then she looks at me. I reach out and brush the hair out of her eyes.

It's like the finest down.

I FOLLOW MALLORY DOWN THE LADDER and outside into the sunlight. We stand there, hundreds of kids moving around us.

I say, "I've gotta look for Couch."

She says, "I know. I've gotta go home. My Grandma's coming for dinner." She starts to walk away, but she turns back. "That was fun—I'm glad I came."

I say, "Hey, what about this writing group?"

Mallory smiles, moves a step closer. "It'll start in September."

"Oh." I nod. "Tony Jones should be showing up at my place after supper—if you want to come by."

"Maybe," she says.

"I've gotta go look for Couch."

"I've gotta get home."

I watch her disappear into the crowd.

HE'S GOT TO BE AROUND HERE SOMEWHERE. This should be when being tall pays off. I push my way to the edge of the crowd—why's everyone standing around?—and I stand there, start to circle, circle.

"Couch!" I call out a few times. Then I see him. Already on his bike and almost to the corner at the end of the block.

It seems to take forever to unlock my bike, wrestle it from all the legs of all the people, then I'm away down the street after him. "Couch!"

I see a flash of green cap and yellow ponytail around the next corner and I follow, but Couch is fast. I have to work to keep up. The green cap goes around another corner and another. To no place in particular, it seems. Just away from me. Even though I haven't seen him look back once, I know he knows I'm on his trail.

He heads out towards the dike now, and I follow up the steep grassy slope leading off the road. He's still ahead, spewing gravel from the path that runs alongside the river and borders the marsh. He's riding hard, out of his seat, the rear wheel skittering...and then down he goes and I'm on him in five seconds.

And what am I going to say?

The river tide is high. I always have an urge to jump in when the water's so close.

"Why'd you ruin my plywood?" I ask.

He shrugs, pulls himself to his feet. Winces. He must've pulled or twisted something. "Guess you couldn't use the wood after all, eh? Not till you paint over it, get rid of the poet stuff!" Couch laughs, but it's a miserable sound. He picks up his bike. "I might've ruined your wood," he says, "but you've ruined everything!"

"Everything?"

"Yeah. How it used to be. Riding and T.C. with Dad and hockey camp every summer." He steps closer to me and sticks his finger in my face. "You're not coming, are you? And you can't even tell me. But I know. You're not coming to camp."

"No," I say. "I told you—I don't have the money."

"It's not about money," he says.

"You're right. It's not. I'm not a hockey player."

It *is* easy to lie. But it feels good to admit to something, too. "Really," I say, "I just don't want to go to hockey camp this year."

"But we go every year."

"I didn't even like it last year." Wow. I haven't realized this until now, with the words popping out of my mouth.

Couch is staring at me. "What else are you keeping secret?" His eyes narrow. "That time in the hallway when Ms. P said you were coming round to English, and you shrugged. You said it was nothing. You lied then."

Couch is the jury and the judge all at once, and I'm the guilty one. I could stand up for not going to camp, but this is different. That is, I want to come clean, but suddenly it doesn't feel easy or good.

"I lied another time too." I can hardly raise my voice.

Couch steps even closer.

"When I let you think my broken leg was from a skiing accident," I say.

Couch frowns as his memory does a bit of time travel.

"Back then?" he says. "You lied back then?"

I nod.

"What else is there, Kidd? What else? You're some package deal yourself!" He's starting to turn away now, but he continues speaking. "There is another time, isn't there?"

"What other time?"

"Your *emergency* you had to run to."

He means Roland. "It was an emergency," I say.

Couch straddles his bike. "That's what you keep saying, but how do I know it's the truth?" He starts to ride back the way we came.

"It *was* an emergency!" I shout after him. "That's the truth!"

"Yeah, yeah. I know all about it. The *girl* on the phone. Your mum told me everything!"

This time I don't follow him. I watch him go and wait until he's out of sight before I leave for home.

How could Mum have told him everything? Mum doesn't know everything.

MUM'S DOING SURGERY on an ancient chair.

"Mum," I say. "When Couch called here on Tuesday, what did you tell him?"

"Tuesday?" Mum's forehead goes wrinkly. "Tuesday. I told him a girl called, and you went out...."

She says something else, but I'm already racing for the phone.

Their answering machine is on. He's not home yet.

I start for the door. Tony Jones could be here any minute.

No. Back to the phone. Listen all the way through Mr. F's long message. Then, "Couch? Look, man, I'm sorry. I didn't know Mum told you it was a girl who called Tuesday night. You gotta believe me. It wasn't a girl. It was Roland's mum. She was worried about him. It's not like you think...." What else can I say? Oh.

"And I did use the wood. No thanks to you. Tony Jones can think what he wants." I stop and then go on. Couch's answering machine cuts off recording if there's too much silence. "I did write a poem. I might even write more!" I say. "That's part of my package deal too." I begin to hang up, then add, "Just get over here, man! Tony Jones might be showing up."

After a shower—it's about time—I go out to wait on the half-pipe.

DINNER TIME COMES AND GOES. Quarter to seven, Mum brings a sandwich and tells me the time, which is right on my wrist but I've been trying hard not to look at it. The tuna sandwich is good. I'd like another, but now I'm getting stubborn about waiting. I ride for awhile. I feel like I have room to move with the extension. But the bigness feels empty, so I sit some more. Wait. The sky begins to grow dark. He's not going to come. Street lamps are turned on. Shadows from the cedars move. Mum brings me a sweater.

I think about all the times that Mum has brought me a sweater because I'm out so late. When I was little and even now. I put it on the plywood beside me and shiver.

Our street is not a main street. The only traffic is cars that belong to people who live here, so at eight in the morning there is a rush of leavings, and five-thirty has always been the worst time for street hockey. Other than that, it's a quiet street, especially on late spring evenings. Like this one. I hear silence. Then a faint whirring sound, a buzz. It disappears for a split second, a gentle thumping sound, then buzzzzzz. Silence, thump, buzzzzz.

Now I know. Jones! And he's curb hopping. Silence, thump, buzzzzz. I hear a voice:

"582! Is that you, 582? This is Collingwood Crescent, isn't it?"

Someone—Who Else?—rummages in the cedars. "Hallo! 582!"

"Jones!" I say.

"Are you the Kidd at 582?" He's grinning.

"That's me!"

shakespeare

"THIS IS SOMETHING!" SAYS TONY JONES, and I almost laugh out loud. "This is something" is a phrase Grandma used to say.

Jones wheels the platform slowly. "Radical!" he says now. Okay. That's more like it. He grins at me suddenly. "The show went all right today, don't you think, Kidd?"

I nod, but he's already turned away, working up a bit of speed to the far platform.

"You make this yourself?" he shouts over his shoulder.

"Yes," I say loudly. Pause. "The extension, anyway." Pause again. "A friend...and his dad...helped with the original."

Jones pedals backwards and stops in front of me. He stands on his bike, and with perfect balance, does a nice, slow peg wheelie. So much for moving too fast to read.

He moves over the front wheel, then rides forward, his foot on a front peg. He coasts. Wavers. Falls forward, drops off the bike, climbs back on. Circling, circling. "Where's your bike, Kidd?"

I go and get it from where it's been leaning against the porch.

"Let's see you ride, 582 Collingwood Kidd."

I don't answer. I just ride and build speed and I can hear Jones on the far side. We're like one of those perfectly weighted desk toys, two steel balls moving exactly opposite, keeping balance, always circling. Then Jones lifts off over one platform and the cedar shadows struggle to grab his shadow and pull it down again. Then it's my turn, and we're together again, each jumping at either end, passing each other, then leaping. Flying at night feels different from the day. Not that I'm moving any higher, but somehow the plywood half-pipe seems farther away beneath me, and the air has a different feel to it, as if the molecules are looser. I can hear Jones's clock-like out-breath as he lands, but I don't know how much time passes.

Jones slows first. He stops, puts the bike down on the grass, then stands for a moment in the middle of the half-pipe before lying down. I keep circling, jumping.

"Don't stop!" he calls out. I don't.

He laughs like a little kid being tickled. "Ha ha! Feel the vibrations! I can feel your tires right through to my bones, Kidd!"

Finally I stop, exhausted, sweating. Jones is still lying in the middle of the plywood. "You've got good stars here," he motions to the sky. "Not like in L.A." He sits up, pulls on the sweater Mum brought me earlier. I sit next to him and we're silent for awhile, except for my panting.

He motions to the extension.

"What's with the POET FREAK stuff?"

"A friend thought he'd decorate my plywood for me." I spin the tire of my bike, lying nearby.

"You a poet?" asks Jones.

In my mind I remember the look on Roland's face as I left him that day, standing in his doorway, behind his mother. That look as if something in him was free now. "Yeah," I say.

Tony Jones nods. "That's cool," he says. He keeps nodding as if I've said that I'm going to buy a new seat for my bike, or some other everyday thing. Like it's nothing special. Definitely nothing out of the ordinary.

"So give me some, Shakespeare Kidd! Give me some poetry."

My mind is suddenly blank. Shakespeare Kidd. That, from Tony Jones.

"You need some inspiration?" he asks.

I pick up my bike, climb on, pedal. Circle him. All right.

At first, I speak softly, just loud enough for him to hear—

> *circle*
> *wheels spin*

And Tony Jones echoes me—

> *air*
> > *air*
> *air*
> > *air*
> *air*
> > *air*

I raise my voice, and each time Tony answers me, I get louder.

I shout—

> *air all around me*
>
> *all around—*

echoes Tony.
Couch pushes through the hedge, Roland be-
hind him.
My bike soars—

> *I'm off*
> > *I'm off*
> *the top*
> > *the top*
> *body against the sun*

Then Roland yells. Scares me—

> *turn away sun!*

My turn—

> *gravity laughs*
>
> *laughs—*

echoes Tony.
Couch scrambles to the top of the new platform and stands with his arms out—

> *hah hah hah hah*

The sound is almost cruel.
My bike is flying. Tony stomps up and down the

length of the stained glass plywood. Couch keeps his place on the cliff. Roland stands to the side.

I go on—

> *reel me in gravity*
> *reel!!*

Couch reels an invisible line and draws me flying toward him—

> *reel, Kidd!*

Then I'm moving down again—

> *pass the summit*

Roland knows the poem. In an ominous voice, he says—

> *drop drop*

And I say—

> *feet   knees   stomach   pedals   MOVE*

Couch must've read more than he'll admit—

> *RUSH!*

I fly up the ramp—

> *rubber hum buzzzzzzzzzz*

Then up the far end—

push up   up   up

And they echo me.
Tony—

UP

Roland—

UP

And Couch—

UP

I cry out—

AIR BORN!

My wheels slow. I stop.
It's very quiet.
Couch doesn't come down. He sits on the edge up there, apart. Roland steps onto the plywood though, and hands something to Tony.
"This is for you."
It's a tie of course. Stripes of bright yellow, red, and green. Tony Jones puts it around his neck and tightens the knot that Roland has already tied for him.
And more silence.
Tony slowly takes off the sweater, hands it to me, then sticks out his hand and shakes mine.
"Bye, Shakespeare," he says. "Keep rolling the wheels and the words."

He looks up at Couch and motions to the graffiti.

"You the painter?"

Couch nods.

"Maybe come to L.A. some day and do mine."
Tony picks up his bike.

He high-fives Roland and waves at Couch, who scrambles down and wipes his hand on the back of his pants before offering it to his hero for a shake. Seems Couch is speechless.

Then Tony Jones is gone, through the hedge; his tires buzz down the block. The cedars hardly move after him, and seconds later, it's as if he's never been here, on my moonscape.

I pull the sweater on, still warm from the best freestyler in the world, and my stomach roars for food. I've forgotten to eat. Maybe Mum's left something in the fridge.

Couch and Roland are sitting on the edge of the half-pipe, their shoulders touching.

"I'll bring some food out."

I go in the house, which feels kind of different, and I don't quite know why. It has something to do with Jones, I know, but even though I'm a fan—probably his second biggest after Couch—I don't know why I should feel so different. I shrug as I open the fridge door and feel the cold. I mean, my life isn't going to change because I rode with Tony Jones, is it? I close the door, even though I haven't seen what's in the fridge, and haven't taken anything out.

Maybe it's because I said I'm a poet. I finally said it. I said it to Couch, and I shouted it from the half-pipe.

I open the fridge door again. Mum's left a plate of lasagne, wrapped in a plastic bag, with a note taped to it. *Gone to the movies. Microwave 3 minutes. Love you.* I didn't even notice when she left.

The microwave whirs, and I look through the window at my friends outside.

Ding. I take the lasagne out, cut it in three, put it on three chipped plates and go outside. I hand one to Couch and one to Roland. Couch sniffs it and breaks off a bit with the side of his fork. He tastes it.

Roland eats.

"So you did make the extension," Couch says. "I didn't think you'd really live with the poet thing. I thought you'd paint over it no matter what." The look on his face is sudden and approving. "I thought you'd hide it, but you didn't." He looks at his bright painting. "Maybe I did overdo it a bit."

"A bit," I say. "And you worried for nothing."

"Yeah?"

"Yeah."

"I thought maybe you'd end up in some special class. Or your mum would want to send you away to another school. Stuff seems to be happening with you." He laughs like a bark, then gathers up one of his knees in his arms and rests his chin on it. His eyes half close. "What was Mallory...doing at the gym today?" He looks wary suddenly.

I shrug. "I guess she thought she'd check out what we were talking about."

He nods. "I didn't expect to see her there. 'Specially when she looked like she was liking it. I didn't think she'd ever like sports. Or even notice anyone who likes sports...." His voice kind of drifts off, and I realize something that I'm not sure I'm supposed to.

"You like Mallory Nightingale," I say before I can stop myself.

"I used to wonder about her. That was all though," he adds quickly. "She likes you. That's cool."

Roland looks up from his plate. Looks at Couch. Looks at me.

I can hear squabbling starlings.

"Geez, Couch. I didn't know."

He shrugs. "I didn't tell you." His fingers are poking at his face.

Roland begins to eat again, chewing as if he hasn't had food in days. He waves his fork at the half-pipe, and between bites, says, "Your tattoo plans are pretty good, Couch. But this—this painting— is *big*."

"You think? 'COUPLET KIDD'—I 'specially like that one." Couch talks with his mouth full and pokes at Roland's side. "The weird thing is, I kind of liked doing it..."

"I'll bet you did!"

"No, really. I did." He looks at me quickly. "And I know what you're thinking—that I enjoyed it because I was angry about your poem and you turning into some kind of dream boy. But no. Who knows? Maybe I'll be a graffiti artist or some kind of painter. When I'm retired from the NHL, of course. Man, if you can write poetry, I guess I can paint."

He chews. "This stuff isn't too bad."

two shadows

I LEAVE MY CURTAINS OPEN AGAIN. I find it hard to end this day. I'm still awake when I hear Mum come in the front door quietly and hang up her coat. She pauses outside my door as she always does, always has. I hear her fingertips brush my door before she goes to her own room.

I move from my bed to the window where the light from the street is almost bright enough to read. Bright enough to write. I close the window—the spring air is cool—and as I do, there's a rustle of paper under my feet: a paper airplane. I unfold it.

> *Og—*
> *Grandma had lots of stories tonight.*
> *Sorry I couldn't make it. See you on*
> *Monday.*
> > *—Mal*

The carpenter's pencil is still in the pocket of my jeans, now crumpled on the bed. I reach for the pencil, and a piece of paper from the desk. Through the window, I can still see the half-pipe.

I can't make out the words in the shadow of the hedge but I know what they say.

I smooth the paper on the sill and write:

> *it's*
> *wild in the street—*
> *light on the moon.*
>
> *ping*
> *um*
>
> *two shadows j*
> *through holes in the cheese*
> *looking for the old man*
> *looking to fly off the end of that long pointed*
> *nose*
> *spinning like quarters on the*
> *half-*
> *pipe moon.*

Two shadows. Jones and me. Grandpa and me. Couch. Roland. Mallory. I put the paper on the table beside my bed, and place Great Uncle John's tie over it. Tomorrow, I'll ask Roland to teach me how to knot that tie.

ABOUT THE AUTHOR

ALISON ACHESON's first juvenile novel, *Thunder Ice*, was published by Coteau Books in 1996. With a brother who is a freestyle BMX rider, she was able to do some thorough research on the topic. Alison writes poetry and fiction for adults as well, and has appeared in *Grain* magazine, *The Antigonish Review*, and *Arc*. Alison holds a degree in creative writing from the University of British Columbia and has lived her whole life in the lower mainland.

ABOUT THE ILLUSTRATOR

WARD SCHELL is an artist-in-residence at the Neil Balkwill Civic Arts Centre in Regina, where he teaches drawing, painting, and cartooning. Ward received his art education at the Emily Carr Institute of Art & Design in Vancouver and at the University of Regina. He recently created the colour illustrations for *Thunder Ice*, and *Jess and the Runaway Grandpa*, two other Coteau Books novels for young readers.